By ERIC ARVIN

Another Enchanted April
Azrael and the Light Bringer
Galley Proof
Grand Adventures (Dreamspinner Anthology)
Kid Christmas Rides Again
The Mingled Destinies of Crocodiles and Men
The Rascal
The Rest Is Illusion
Simple Men
Slight Details & Random Events (Author Anthology)
Terms We Have for Dreaming
Wave Goodbye to Charlie
Woke Up in a Strange Place

SUBSURDITY SERIES
SubSurdity
Suburbilicious
SuburbaNights

Published by DREAMSPINNER PRESS
www.dreamspinnerpress.com

The Rascal

ERIC ARVIN

DREAMSPINNER PRESS

Published by

DREAMSPINNER PRESS

5032 Capital Circle SW, Suite 2, PMB# 279, Tallahassee, FL 32305-7886 USA
www.dreamspinnerpress.com

The Rascal
© 2017 Eric Arvin.

Cover Art
© 2015 Adrian Nicholas.
Cover content is for illustrative purposes only and any person depicted on the cover is a model.

ISBN: 978-1-63533-822-5
Digital ISBN: 978-1-63533-823-2
Library of Congress Control Number: 2017904065
Published April 2017
v. 2.0
First Edition published by Wilde City Press, October 2015.

Printed in the United States of America

This paper meets the requirements of
ANSI/NISO Z39.48-1992 (Permanence of Paper).

PEOPLE WOULD believe almost anything if told to them by the right storyteller. But would anyone believe what he had been through in the past few months? Would they believe his life story? One can believe in angels. Those, the world has said, are acceptable spiritual flourishes. But tell someone of ghosts, of demons—and vengeful ones at that—and you're a crazy man.

The fall should have killed him. That was the whole point. But he lay there, his cheek against the moist earth at the bottom of the well while something sharp and jagged jabbed angrily at his stomach from beneath him. At least it didn't hurt. He was beyond that kind of pain.

He'd never known darkness as black as this. Yet there was moonlight somewhere above him. He just couldn't bend his neck to see it. He was so far down the well the moon had given up its search for him. Any other person would have tried to scream. To cry and shout for help, even if in vain.

He heard dripping, water seeping through the stones of the well and soaking into the garbage around him. Into this, his eventual final resting place. He wondered how long he would have to wait for death. The horrible hours waiting. How long had he waited already?

A strange whistling could be heard faintly overhead. Night breezes on the coast were the loneliest in all the world. They bit at the ears. There were certain things—certain voices and laughter—he would have loved to hear one last time before he died, but those winds… he wanted no part of them. Those winds brought trouble on their currents. He'd felt that harsh tinge to them, that pinch, not long after he had bought the place. Or rather, not long after his wife had bought the place.

If she had only known the truth, everything could have been avoided.

His mind was clouding now. He felt a trickle of water on his face. No. Not water. Blood. Most likely his own from the fall. He imagined himself a twisted mess on the stinking well floor with all the other tossed debris from decades past. Just the latest addition to a pile of refuse, out of sight and out of mind. Don't think about it and it doesn't exist.

He imagined he was smiling, though he couldn't be certain. There was no way the rascal could get him now. He had felt it trying for weeks, every hour more intrusive since the dreams began.

He hadn't known what it was in the beginning. At first it had been but an itch. But as things went on, the power of possession grew stronger. It slid beneath his skin like he was an old shirt and it was a familiar fit. The rascal was taking control of things. What it wanted was blood and flesh. And it knew his flesh very well. Oh yes. Very well, indeed.

He, a modern man with his family, had come, shrugging off anything he was told about the old place, casting all warnings aside as superstitious hokum. He only wanted to do his penance. But then it began.

He had never tried to understand the reasons why this dark thing wanted him. All he knew was that it desired the body he walked around in, the four limbs and aging flesh. And it would have had it if he had not done something drastic to stop it.

But now where was the rascal? Did it not want this broken man on the well floor? Could it not reanimate his limbs and climb up out of the well as he had seen the damned thing reanimate his precious little—?

He could wish he had never come here to this place, but that was useless now. He could cry. He most likely already was. Again, however, what good was crying over a fate he brought on himself?

The lines were blurring. Things were spreading apart at molecular levels. He heard a low moan and he felt his dying heart jump. He thought it was the rascal at first, climbing down the well to take him over after all. But that could not be true. The dark hate had released him as he threw himself down the well. No. The moan was something more familiar. And then he realized what was happening. This was his own soul crying. Leaving for good.

"Don't go! Don't leave me here in this cold place all alone." How like a child every man is at the end. How greedily he clings to some sort of comfort.

But it was a slippery thing to catch, his soul. Like a fish wriggling in wet hands. The soul climbs up regardless of cage or coercion.

He did not suffer much longer in loneliness and pain. His eyes shut. The last visual image he would have of the world was the glimmer of a little glass pony his daughter had thrown away months ago.

ON BAD LUCK HILL

THE TOWN of Wicker sat like an awestruck supplicant below the hill. The quaint little structures—the churches and banks, the Italianate stores, and restaurants of Main Street—even seemed to lean slightly away in veneration. The height of each successive building shrunk as they neared the hill. Both sides of the street were like lines of perspective in a painting, leading the eyes straight off to what would seem Wicker's raison d'être.

Chloe Singh-Cane felt the town's sense of reverence and expectation as she walked from the old, beaten Jeep into the small grocery store with her husband, Jeff. The few people on the sidewalks abruptly stopped what they were doing and looked at the strangers as if in rapt gratitude. Their expressions verged on hunger. Chloe walked as close to Jeff as he would allow her. His personal space was still precious to him where she was involved.

The store clerk, a razor-thin woman with willows for fingers, watched them from beneath the rims of her glasses. A pleasant, if knowing smile never shifted or fell. There was no one else in the store.

It was a small cubicle of a shop that had been there since the town's founding. Like all of the structures on the main street, it seemed stoic and stuck, as if the shelves and walls were still adjusting to fluorescent lighting and the computer age was but science fiction. Arts and crafts were sold alongside loaves of bread and bags of candy. Individual colas could still be purchased out of an icebox. There was a smell of nostalgic comfort: wood stoves and wax candles.

Jeff went to the pharmacy aisle and picked up a bottle of aspirin. It had been a long drive, and his back was hurting him.

Chloe had volunteered to take over, but he shrugged her off as if her suggestion was an annoyance.

Chloe wandered around the store, happy to stretch her legs. She was still surrounded by silence, but at least this was a new silence. In the Jeep, Jeff's silence had been covered by rock music. In the store, it was disguised by pop-flavored piano music and scented candles. She picked up a bag of candy corn and a bag of sour gummies.

Jeff was waiting at the cash register. He had a cold bottle of root beer to wash down the aspirin. The clerk put down the tabloid magazine she was thumbing through and continued to smile at them as she rang the items up. The lighting behind her caused her long fingers to cast thin shadows.

"Just passing through?" she asked, her voice a scratchy, nicotine-lined thing.

"No," Chloe offered. "We bought a cottage up on the hill."

The clerk's bagging of the items slowed to a crawl. Her eyes swallowed them. "The little place up on Bad Luck Hill?"

"Is that what it's called? Why in heaven's name is it called Bad Luck Hill?"

The clerk's item bagging picked up. "Silly reasons. Or none at all. Who can remember how things get their names?"

Jeff and Chloe exchanged quick glances. It was the first eye contact with Jeff Chloe could remember having for miles.

"I'm Odette," the wiry woman said. "Me and my sister, Alma, run this place. You let us know if you need anything else, you hear? We can get you anything you need."

Jeff picked up the small brown paper bag, rolling it at the top. "How close is the next town?" he asked. "Is there a hospital near?"

"Do you need one?"

"Just inquiring. This is the first town we've seen for an hour and a half."

"There's your answer, sweet pea. We're it as far as Bad Luck Hill is concerned. As for a hospital, that's an hour farther still. But we got a doctor, Doc Holland. He's good. Self-trained."

"Self-trained," Jeff repeated in a whisper.

"We should be going," Chloe said. "We have a lot to unpack. We don't want to keep you."

Odette snorted. "Keep me from what, sweet pea? Look around. We're not exactly Walmart. You're the first customers we've had all day."

Chloe gave a pleasant, if uncomfortable smile and touched Jeff's shoulder to suggest they should leave. They had made it to the door when Odette turned their heads again.

"But things will pick up. Our business here at the store, I mean. Business is gonna pick up right quick very soon. I can sense these things."

Winter was coming. The winds were pushing it over the sea to the coast. From the passenger seat, Chloe dissected the sky and the sea as they drove the twisting incline road to their new home, a place they had purchased sight unseen. Chloe tried to peer past the dulling grays. She tried to find the point where sea touched sky, both born of the same line yet separating in opposite directions. The gray would not let her, though. It was too gray, too uncertain it was even a color.

Jeff drove. He hadn't said anything for a good twenty minutes, not since they left Wicker. Jeff had always been the quiet sort. It was a selfish quiet, as if his time and words were gold and he would not spend either hastily. But that could no longer be the go-to reasoning for all of his reserve. For the past year, things had changed between them, fallen away, and that was all Chloe's doing. She realized her error and owned it the best she could. That was one of the reasons she had mentioned moving somewhere else in the first place. New beginnings could only take root in new ground. Maybe Chloe's apologies would be heard better on stranger earth. And, too, it would be good for them—for their relationship—to get out of the reaches of her family. They were born meddlers. Her father was an Indian businessman; her mother, an American entrepreneur who owned the adventure tourism business that employed both her and Jeff.

"Why would you need that much time off?" her mother had asked when Chloe told her they were moving. "You can work just as well there as you can here, can't you? And where is there, anyway? Maybe it could be a new business opportunity for us."

"No, Mother. No business. Just me and Jeff. And I'm not telling you where we're moving."

"I can find you easily enough, darling."

"Mother, no. And I have a new cell phone. So does Jeff. The old number is useless. Just let us be for a while."

"Alright. Fine. But you'd better work this out, missy. Jeff's a fine man. Maybe better than you deserve. Buying a place without even going to look at it first. That's just asking for a whole heap of trouble."

It might have been foolish to purchase the little cottage without visiting it first. They had been told this by everyone, not just Chloe's know-it-all mother. Technically, though, they had seen it. There were some lovely, if not professional photographs on the Internet. The cottage was a tiny thing. As quaint and inviting as any fairytale home, it was surrounded by large, vibrant trees. The place looked a bit unloved and neglected in the photograph, and the photographer had evidently not cleared the shot because there was the shadow of a figure staring back from the front window, but the agent they were dealing with (Donna Tharp, "a trusted name in realty," according to the ads) told them everything could be easily fixed or sewn up.

"You'll love it! Just love it! Hand to God." Chloe didn't like that last bit of Donna Tharp's statement. It came very close to blasphemy.

They had yet to speak to the previous owner of the cottage. She still lived on the hill above them in a large house that overlooked the cliff, threatening to throw itself—every last splinter—over the edge. Donna Tharp had told Chloe that the previous owner had never actually lived in the cottage, and Chloe saw why from her seat in the Jeep. She could see the big house on the cliff before she had even gotten the first true glance at the cottage in the woods. The sad foreboding structure sent a chill through her. She hoped the same despondency was not prevalent at the cottage.

They were on a bumpy gravel drive once they finally got off the main highway. It led them under large trees and through deep puddles, and all the while it was up, up, up. Chloe hoped they would get to the cottage before too much longer. Images of horror films and cannibalistic families living in the woods ran through her mind. She knew not to look out her passenger side window. She knew to keep her eyes locked straight ahead when her "feelings" came on as strong as this, especially in wooded areas. She might sense something she would rather not. Chloe had a feeling for things. She felt more deeply than others the things that the world would call supernatural. She turned to God to help her in dealing with this gift. There were all sorts of sins out there. All manner of sinners. Her senses were always very keen. She had "feelings" often. But for the most part, she had trained herself not to see. That was the key. Just don't see it.

They drove through a creek bed that ran shallow. No Hope Creek was the overwrought name Donna Tharp had given her for the place. The rocks knocked against the tires of the Jeep. It wasn't a huge creek, but in the winter it might be trouble with the wrong vehicle. Chloe noticed the density of trees grew thicker as they crossed No Hope Creek. Crossed it right on up to Bad Luck Hill. The trees across the creek seemed more interested in the Jeep now. They clawed at it as the vehicle climbed. Chloe almost said something about them to take her mind off the silence. (The radio had become a storm of fuzz some ways back.) When she looked to Jeff, however, a smile was creeping across his handsome face.

"What's funny?" Chloe asked.

"I think this was a great idea," Jeff said. "I think I'll like it here."

That was all it took to dispel any doubts she had harbored about the move or certainly about the nosy trees and cannibalistic families. Jeff's smile meant that everything was going to be okay after all. He smiled so rarely these days.

The trees on Chloe's side disappeared once more as the Jeep made the ascent. They fell away to reveal a sharp drop to the sea. The cottage was tucked into the woods on the driver's side a good ways up the hill, and it faced the cliff. As she got out of the Jeep, Chloe noticed first the descending rocks to the sea below before she saw anything of the cottage. These were big rocks, every one of them a brain smasher. The cottage, in juxtaposition, was a harmless and fragile thing.

The place was in desperate need of some color or at least a new coat of white. Weeds grew around it like tiny bullies, but there was evidence of wildflowers too. The big house could be seen up the hill from the cottage's small porch. Jeff was already looking around the back of the cottage. Chloe, though, was halted there on the porch. There was a sense of something. Something in the window. Like the figure in the first photograph that had brought the cottage to her attention. A wave of chills ran down her back, and she hugged herself. She chose not to look any farther than the porch until Jeff came back around to meet her. She'd enter the cottage when he did.

"It's just the moving-day jitters," she whispered. The lines between sea and sky blurred in the distance.

"There's a barn out back," Jeff said as he rounded the corner of the cottage. He spoke with an excitement Chloe had not heard since their first trips as adventure tour guides together. "There's a bunch of slabs and timber stacked in it, but nothing else that I could see. There looks to be something in front of the barn too. It's covered by a big stone. Maybe a well."

Jeff let himself into the cottage. Chloe still held tight to herself. The front door was unlocked as Miss Donna Tharp had told them it would be. As promised, the place came fully furnished. Neither Chloe nor Jeff knew much about antiques— they were adventure sports recreationists, after all—but they knew "old" when they saw it.

As they lifted the thick plastic protective sheets, Chloe looked at Jeff. "Call the Antiques Roadshow. We'll make a mint."

The cottage was small and cozy. A large mantel and fireplace were the focal point of the living area. A small, ancient TV sat insignificantly on a stand. A scratched coffee table, a rocking chair, and a worn but comfortable couch rounded out the room's furnishings. A kitchen connected directly to the living area just past the couch. Deeper in the cottage, down a narrow hallway, was a bedroom. There were no trinkets or personal knickknacks left behind from the last inhabitants of the cottage. And it was strange, but Chloe had half expected there to be some evidence that someone was still living there. It was just a feeling she had, one she couldn't shake, and one brought on by the feeling she had encountered on the porch.

Chloe drifted from room to room, carefully pulling away the plastic sheeting to reveal the old treasures or junk beneath them. The sound of the stiff plastic was similar to that of an ocean wave, though stirring dust instead of dirty seagulls. Chloe found her way to the bedroom. Jeff had gone to the kitchen, stripping, ripping, and tearing the old furnishings of their plastic shielding as he went. The force with which he tore the sheeting away reverberated through the cottage, putting Chloe on edge.

She found a bureau in the bedroom and uncovered it as delicately as she could to combat her husband's violence. The dark wood was warped in areas and could have used a new finish. Two brass knobs were missing, and the bottom drawer looked to be crooked. All the same, it would serve its purpose. So much of the furniture would keep her and Jeff busy fixing and sanding and readjusting. She sighed in relief at this thought. They wouldn't have time to think about other things.

The drawers were cranky and stubborn, but Chloe managed to eventually open and inspect them one by one. Decades-old scent of staleness and moths overcame her to the point that she backed away for a moment. They were all empty but for the crooked bottom one. Therein lay a small assemblage of photographs. Chloe gathered them up and shuffled them neatly. They were old black and whites, some torn and bug-eaten, all stained by time and neglect. They looked like photographs from a movie magazine. These were scenes of the adored glitterati at fabulous parties by large pools. Scenes of excess given respectability by black and white. Chloe recognized some of those in the photographs. They were movie stars, most of them still living, but way past their prime now. She didn't know many of their names, but she knew their faces. Everyone did. She had seen a film or two every now and then. The world was all about entertainment these days. About selling one's business and selling out one's past.

"Look at this," she said to Jeff, thinking he had come into the room with her. There was that discernible dimming of light by shadow, as if someone was behind her in the doorway. She didn't bother to look up from the photographs, mesmerized by their glamour. Then there was a whisper, a breeze, like a door had been left ajar and an uncomfortable cool wind had been let into the room.

Only when Jeff answered from the other side of the small house ("Did you say something?"), did Chloe look up, startled. Jeff was not in the room with her at all. There was no one in the doorway as she had thought. She swallowed back a prickling fear and caught the wisp of a "feeling." The chills ran through her again, and she closed the drawer and left the bedroom, photographs in hand. Strangely enough, thoughts of burrowing beetles filled her mind. The creepy crawling nightmares of childhood.

She found Jeff standing in the kitchen, staring out the back door toward the little red barn. She approached and touched him on the shoulder. The wood floor creaked below her. He didn't move.

"Are you okay?" Jeff asked. If his voice held any true concern, Chloe couldn't hear it. He was detached. Mentally, he was somewhere outside by the barn.

"I'm fine," she said. In his arms, if he would ever hold her again, she could shake off the nightmares the "feelings" gave her. "Why don't we go introduce ourselves to the woman on the hill before we unpack? We're to be neighbors. It's best to get off on good footing."

Jeff at last turned his attention to her and nodded at the photographs she held to her chest. "Pictures?"

"Yes. I found them in a drawer. They're interesting. Whoever lived here before seems to have had an interesting life."

Jeff examined them. "Or maybe they were just fans. You can find memorabilia at any swap shop these days."

"Maybe…."

Jeff shrugged. Chloe saw the look of utter disinterest on his face. He might as well have turned to stone. She wanted to scream at him. "Pay attention to me! See me again!" She felt the urge to grab him and shake him. To bait an argument if only to have him look at her with some sort of passion in his eyes. Yes, that was it. That was what she had to do. She was going to do it. This moment. It had been an awful day. A very uncomfortable awful day and she needed some kind of release. A good sparring match might be just the thing. She breathed in deep and—

Pop pop pop!

Three shots came from up on the hill. Jeff and Chloe stared at one another for a brief second.

"Gunshots?" Chloe asked.

"A rifle," he said.

He quickly walked out the front door, obviously expecting her to follow. Chloe stood for a moment, reining in the anger she had let boil. How could this be a home for them? Already she had planted a seed of resentment. She tried to convince herself everything would turn out right in the end. Yet something within her sounded the creeping crawling again. The burrowing. Jeff called to her from the Jeep, and she jumped and looked out the door. He was at the wheel, ready to go.

The drive to the top of the hill wasn't a long one, easily climbable, if steep. The big house could be seen the whole way. Chloe was already feeling a wariness toward the intrusive structure. Every morning when they woke up, the big house would be watching over them at the cottage. Like it was waiting for something.

"It's going to be a big project, fixing that place up," Jeff said as they wound the curves of the gravel road along the cliff. "But I'm up for it."

"It's falling apart," Chloe said, somewhat less enthused.

"I'm up for it," he reiterated in a tone of voice that told her to push no further. "The little place has been hit by decades of storms. All she needs is a bit of repair and someone to look after her."

"So you've got a new gal in your life?" She regretted the statement the moment she said it. Jeff was silent.

As they neared the big house, a thin figure stood at the bottom of the broad porch steps. She was dressed in black, her hands clasped in one another. The house, rising self-importantly behind and above her, echoed her form. There might have been life there in the big house once, but no more. At least, none present on the outside. It lumbered in its aged regality.

They had been told that the lady in the house never went down past the cottage. Not even to head into Wicker. She had her groceries and anything she needed brought up from town and left on the porch, where she would retrieve them. They had been told this by Donna Tharp.

"She's a strange woman," Donna Tharp had said. "You probably won't want to know her. I wouldn't."

Cautiously, Chloe and Jeff looked at one another, then got out of the car and walked up the hill toward the woman. She had not moved. She was pale but still held an aging beauty. Chloe recognized the woman from the photographs she had found. She would have recognized her without them. While Chloe did not love cinema, she knew enough people who did, and Lana Pruitt was one of the great modern recluses, having retired years ago in her prime. Donna Tharp had not said Lana Pruitt was the cottage's previous owner.

The breeze played with Lana's blonde and silver curls as if on cue. A film effect.

"I saw you from the telescope on the widow's walk," the woman said. Her voice was a recognizable shade of its former glory, deepened by age.

Chloe glanced at the top of the big house. The widow's walk was like a perch for a caged bird. Lana still had not moved even as Chloe stood in front of her, smiling and giving introductions. Lana's gaze rested on Jeff, who stood farther back, near the Jeep. The gulf that existed between Jeff and Chloe was shockingly evident at times.

"So why do they stay together?" Lana whispered.

"Excuse me?" Chloe had been telling the retired actress— lying to her—about how lovely she thought the big house was.

Lana reversed her gaze back to Chloe. "I've set some tea for us on the porch. I thought you might like some after your long trip."

"That would be nice. Thank you."

"Let's not let it get cold, then." Lana turned, movement at last, and slowly made her way up stone-and-wood steps to the porch. Chloe followed. Jeff came last, hands in pockets.

The wind was growing stronger now. There was no humidity in it. It slapped at their faces. The treeless heights on which the big house sat did nothing to keep the abuse from them. The woods only began near the cottage.

"It's very quiet here," Chloe said as they climbed.

"Disturbingly so sometimes. I refuse to hang chimes of any kind. The wind would shake them useless, I'm afraid, and keep me wide awake."

As they climbed, Chloe noticed the house looked less foreboding with each step. Instead, it became desolate and pleading. Paint chipped from its sides like leaves from a tree. The wind shook the windows in their frames so that the house seemed to shake and sigh in despair. To one side of the house was what, at one time, must have been a stunning piece of garden and yard. It was now grown over, though. Thick vines and an army of weeds would not give back the statuary and walkway. There was a fatigued beauty to the scene. It expressed a rotted class. Above it, as was the case all around, the sky was a blighted white, and where it met the sea, there was an indifferent fusion.

The place settings at the table were meticulous and lovely. They were like ornaments from a different, wealthier dollhouse. The china gleamed as Lana Pruitt poured Chloe and Jeff each a cup of tea, then one for herself. There was a tray of sugar cookies in the center of the table. They would not be touched, however. And there were no napkins. The wind that circled the big house forbade them.

Chloe saw a rifle leaning against the house by the door.

"Don't worry," Lana said. "That's not for you. It's for all the damn nuisances that crawl up the hill."

"Nuisances?"

"Pests." Lana said no more about it. She took a sip of her tea.

After a few moments of dangerous silence, but for the wind and the water down below as it crashed on the rocks, Chloe couldn't take it anymore. The silence was intent on driving her mad today. "It's a lovely day... a lovely place."

"Don't invite me to the cottage," Lana said. It was blunt, but not mean.

"What? I didn't mean—"

"I won't come. I haven't been past the tree line on the hill in years. I've never set foot in the cottage, and I don't intend to."

Chloe looked at Jeff. He seemed undisturbed by the actress, but he was studying her. As if she wasn't real and he was looking for a trick to the illusion.

"Never? But there are pictures...."

Lana gave her a suddenly interested glare.

"Old pictures of you and...."

"Oh, those." The actress waved her hand dismissively. "My husband spent a lot of time in the little place with my daughter." She stopped and quickly took another sip of tea. "He fixed it up for her. You know, like a playhouse."

"Quite a playhouse." It was the first thing Jeff had said.

Lana made a gesture as if swatting away the conversation. "Other things," she said. "There are other things you should know about the cottage."

Shadows, Chloe wanted to say. Are there shadows? But she said nothing. She wanted to believe that it was simply nerves for just a little bit longer so that all her plans would not be for naught.

Lana continued. "The barn out back is very old. Maybe too old. It might need to be demolished altogether. There's a well in front of it. I think there is a stone that covers its mouth now, but just know it's there. Be careful." She looked at Jeff. It was a strange look of warning.

"I'll never need the place," Chloe said. "The barn, I mean. That's Jeff's domain if he wants to do something with it."

Lana's eyes flicked back to Chloe. "Be careful."

The tea was finished soon after, but not nearly soon enough for Chloe. Jeff looked back at the actress as they descended the steps. Chloe chose to keep looking straight ahead. Neither of them spoke until they were in the Jeep.

"What a strange woman, don't you think?" Chloe finally spoke. "What an odd woman."

LANA STOOD in front of the tea table, one arm wrapped around a porch pole. She watched the new cottage owners drive back down the hill. She knew they were still watching her in their mirrors. That was good. As long as they watched, as long as they kept an eye out, they might be okay. There was nothing more Lana could do for them. That cottage was bad luck, and she felt a twinge of guilt for selling it to them. They seemed like nice enough people.

She walked back into the big house. She'd remember to bring the china in later. She could have hired help for that. There was more than enough money. But then that would mean company, wouldn't it? That would mean attempted conversations and questions. And besides that annoyance, no one would ever agree to stay in the house once they heard the wind on a cold night.

The big house—Clemson it was called when they bought it, though she never referred to it by name—was furnished with strange antiques that at one time had looked beautiful to Lana. Tall chairs with thin backs and tables with claws. Now they looked beaten and even menacing. She refused to touch many of them. The wood was too dark. It seemed to get darker as the years went by and, in turn, darkened the house. Perhaps she could sell all of it and refurnish with simpler things. Things with straight lines and unimaginative curves that didn't beckon to the past. Or perhaps she wouldn't refurnish the place at all.

How many years had it been since her husband, Michael (surname of Kinsar, though Lana never took it), had left her? How many years since their little girl, Rebecca, had fallen off the cliff? It had all happened soon after they had moved to the big house. The story Michael had told her about that day Rebecca fell had given her chills for years to come. Mad, quaking chills. And then he left too, without a word or a note, that very same year.

The actress wandered—for that was all she did these days: wander and wonder—into her small library, which was no more than a sitting room filled with large books. There was a dusty pink sofa for her to recline on that had been brought up from town in the days she went there. The sofa had originally been part of Rebecca's bedroom furnishings, but Lana brought it into the library after Rebecca had died. She did it herself, pulling it down the stairs against its will. It did not match the other humorless furnishings of the library, but that didn't really matter. No one else ever saw the room.

Lana sat at one of the tables she had declawed and thumbed through a large leather-bound book, a very special book and the only thing in her house she regarded with any importance. Her fingers tingled at the touch of its ancient pages, its obscure script. When she first started the library, she was looking for answers. Now she only searched this one book looking for peace.

ON THAT first night, it was the fiddling that woke her. Or, at least, the remaining echoes of a dream fiddle. At first, Chloe could have sworn it was more distant than a dream. The tune was something fast and amateurish. Something in the trees and speeding, racing through the night air around the cottage and then fading back. Back. Back to where?

Jeff was asleep beside her. His chest rose and fell with each heavy breath. He had once slept through an earthquake on a Peruvian adventure tour they had led together, the trip right before all the troubles began. They did not touch at night while they slept anymore. There was an invisible line down the center of the bed. Chloe felt it every night. It felt like his body heat. It roasted her.

She lay still for a few minutes, wide awake. These were their sheets on this strange bed, but it still did not feel like home. Home seemed a foreign concept now.

Finally, she rose and walked to the kitchen. On nights like this, Chloe was inclined to browse the Internet. Maybe even chat with some friends. But the cottage had yet to provide Internet service, and so her laptop lay closed on the kitchen counter.

She flipped on the light in the helplessly outdated kitchen, searched through a box for her favorite mug and some green tea, and warmed some water up in a saucepan on the antiquated stove. The floor made a ruckus below her as she went from one corner of the room to another. The wood floor, stained by decades of dropped food, gave a louder moan than any other floor in the old cottage. It was a moan that stretched clear across the room. It reached and pleaded. Chloe felt it almost as if it were a pulse beneath her feet. Very old things and very new things, she thought, sounded similar in their whines and wants.

Once the tea was done, she stirred it slowly as she leaned against the counter. Tomorrow she'd start anew. Tomorrow would be the day today was supposed to be. She would begin to repair things, both in the cottage and in her and Jeff's relationship. She took a deep breath and then a small sip. Then she quickly looked toward the kitchen doorway.

Just another trick of the eye, she assured herself. No one is there. You just want someone to be there.

THE COUPLE IN THE COTTAGE

JEFF WALKED to the barn with the first real sense of purpose he'd felt since arriving on Bad Luck Hill. It had been a couple of days, and most of their things were unpacked. That did not feel like purpose to him. Unpacking was mindless. Pick something up. Put it over there. That was it. They had very little of their own furniture, having never really invested in any because neither of them was home very much due to the adventure tourism business. Thankfully, that was not an issue here. The cottage was nicely furnished, if with a style neither Jeff nor Chloe would have ever chosen. Rather, it was something akin to Antique Funereal.

The first evening had been awkward, mirroring the year in that way. But Jeff pushed through it. The house groaned so much while they lay in bed it woke him up a few times. He wondered if Chloe got any sleep at all that first night. Every time he woke up, he could hear her stricken breathing. He kept to his side of the bed, though, as had been the case for the past year. His feelings of contempt for her were somehow stronger that night. The more the autumn winds howled outside, the darker his mind became. Let her shiver alone. Let her think the creaks of the floorboards were monsters, or something worse, sent to drag her to whatever hell she feared the most. In the darker corners of his mind, he knew it was what she deserved anyway. He was relieved when she finally got up and went to the kitchen. It was only then that he was finally able to sleep soundly.

And the dreams he had! They were so vivid. And there was the same strange little boy in every one of them.

The closer Jeff came to the barn, the better he felt. Chloe's pleading shadow was less oppressive. He wondered if she was watching him from the kitchen window at the back of the cottage. Lord, the watching! They were not going to survive as a couple. In the beginning, he thought they might. That if he really tried... but the truth was, he didn't want to try. It was an easy thing to admit, really. It only took two drinks at a bar in Midtown to admit that to himself. And now, after a year and the dread, he knew things would soon fall away between them. Strange, he thought, that they had met because of an adventure sports outfit, running tours to dangerous places for adrenaline junkies. The perception of everyone who knew them was that they could survive anything. Jeff now realized "anything" had a limit.

He opened the barn door and it yawned. If it were a later hour and a dimmer light, that yawn would have sounded more of a warning than a lazy welcome. The small interior of the place was flooded with the light from the opened door. It poured over the stacks and slabs of timber that were piled high. Jeff stood momentarily still and looked over everything. In truth, the little red barn was nothing more than a storage bin. The wood and other remnants of someone else's life had been left to the bugs and the rain and snow when it seeped inside through the planks. The ground was a moist rug of mud and moss. The light peeking through the walls echoed prison bars.

The barn had a strange odor on the inside. Something faint. Something very old and kept way past its prime. It would have been unpleasant if it were any stronger. Jeff swatted at a couple of large black flies that danced around his face. He walked to the nearest pile of wood, taking an armful of the rotted stuff and pitching it outside near the well that lay beneath the large stone. This would be his project. It would be his alone. This barn and the well would be his rescue from the cottage when Chloe became too much. Chloe wouldn't want to spend her time in here. The dankness would make her retch. He had a couple of months before work started again. That was maddening. He couldn't believe now that he had agreed to take some time off to work on something that was already dead. But he could get by with a project. If he could finesse it, this well could save him.

CHLOE WATCHED Jeff walk to the barn. Each footfall resembled more and more the stride of a relieved man. He was relaxed out of her presence. That was very much how she saw him leaving her: relaxing away gradually. There would be no sudden departure or grand good-bye. He would slip away before she knew to scream "Don't leave!"

She held an old photo in her hands, one of the bunch she had found in the crooked drawer in the bedroom. There was Lana Pruitt smiling by a large pool with friends and costars. It was a faded version of what it had once been, yellowed by time and neglect. The images on it were vanishing in a slow magic trick. Lana's face was fainter than the rest, as if someone had touched it repeatedly. Caressed it even. Soon the faces would disappear completely. The bugs and invisible forces of time would eat all the images away as if they had never existed. Transformed from matter to energy. Chloe had heard that once. Everything was matter and energy and fluctuated back and forth that way forever. The Great Indecision of the universe.

Chloe squeezed the edges of the photograph. Things had a way of ripping themselves from your grip just when you think you've got a firm grasp on them. That, she had discovered, was how the world worked. Everything was a tease.

She left the unpacking (there were only a few dishes and framed photographs to find a place for) and walked to the front of the cottage. The rooms still smelled of other people, of stale time, but Chloe was certain that would dissipate.

"God help me if this cottage smells like an old museum forever," she whispered. "God help me."

On the porch, she sat down on the one lonely chair. It wasn't very comfortable and felt near collapse, but it would do for now. They'd get a porch swing in time. There was enough room for that at least.

Her fingers glided over the photograph of Lana Pruitt even as her thoughts danced elsewhere, swirling around the night before. Jeff hadn't stirred when the wind howled and things creaked from inside the house. He'd been awake. She knew that. She'd been with him long enough to be familiar with his quirks. Waking breath and sleeping breath sounded distinctly different. She wondered if her own breathing betrayed her. Could he hear the slight tremor in each of her nighttime breaths?

She had tried to shake the "feelings" off. But now she felt something else: certainty. They were being watched, the both of them. The cottage was doing the watching, she supposed. She did not feel welcome here. Once in the night, she even thought she saw a silhouette in the doorway. She blinked and it was gone. But still, that feeling of otherness in the room had happened too much in the cottage for her to pass off as paranoia. And then, as if sent from somewhere in the air around her, she had heard This will never go away. She did not get much sleep after that.

The wind was picking up off the sea. The daylight was at least some comfort. Light chased away shadows and secrets, had them scurrying to darker corners until twilight. She cradled herself in her sweater, an old college thing that had always brought her solace. But sometimes everything seemed useless against this chill. She couldn't say it was a new chill. It had been between her and Jeff for the past year. But it seemed more formed at the cottage. As if brought more fully to life. Gestating a physicality.

Jeff had found out Chloe had been with another man, some random hookup with a customer on a tour she was leading. Jeff was not on that tour with her. She was drunk and the guy was flirting. One thing led to another, and another led to sex in a tent. He'd reminded her of Jeff, this guy, but she could never remember his name. That was how unimportant he was to her.

Her guilt clawed at her from the inside. Before Jeff found out, Chloe had gone and taken care of the mishap growing inside of her. She couldn't cover it up and say it was Jeff's child. He was unable to give her children due to a trait passed down from his father. That was always a sore point with him. And if Chloe were to admit that she had been with another man….

Jeff should have been none the wiser. An abortion was the only thing to do, so she did it. But something had gone wrong. An infection due to the procedure exposed the whole affair. All the lies and deceit. The wrong choices. Even if she hadn't admitted to cheating, which was impossible given the circumstances, she could see Jeff's eyes. The image he held of her was changed forever. That was when the chill started. That was when it began to feel like an icy wind around her at all times, and the way that chill sounded… it sounded much like the wind from the sea as she sat on the porch in the uncomfortable chair. She hugged herself tighter, bending the old photograph in her hand as it curled into a fist.

"If only I had your willpower, Jeff," she said. "If only I had your determination."

She rose from the chair and walked to the edge of the porch. Her eyes followed the slant of the hill up to the big house. There was the wind-whipped frenzy of cloth from the top of the house, from the widow's walk. Lana was standing there, most likely looking seaward for her lost husband.

"He's never coming back, Lana," Chloe said.

How long had the movie star been alone? It had been years since she had acted in anything. Decades. When did the fans stop showing up looking for her? Or did they even know where to look? When had Lana given up on the world and decided that only a few acres would ever be witness to her years passing?

Chloe looked at the photograph in her hand. "Where's your husband? Why did he leave you?" Perhaps their stories were more similar than Chloe thought.

A violent wind ripped the photograph from her and took it over the cliff and out to sea. Chloe hadn't even the chance to reach for it before it was beyond her grasp.

THEY HAD met on an adventure tour through the Italian Alps. Chloe had taken the job when she was offered it by her mother to get away from the weight of expectation her family placed on her. She was seeking levity. Jeff was seeking the same, only his family was now lame and scattered. His father was dead, his mother was in a coma, and his brother Ethan had been a ward of the state. Nobody expected Jeff to take care of Ethan. Nobody expected it, so he didn't. He took his inheritance money and did some grand adventuring while he still had the time and health to do it. Little did he know it would become his career.

Chloe had been immediately drawn to him. The other eight people in the group were as good as invisible. The moment they met was defined by the sound of the airport terminal where she picked the group up in Italy. Jeff gave her a sly, flirtatious smile and they connected right there over the noise of American tourists and Italian customs officials. She remembered his name. She didn't even have to repeat it to herself as she had with the others on the tour.

"Be professional," she reminded herself. "Don't show favoritism."

"I'm going to date her," Jeff told one of the other tourists. "Then I'm going to marry her."

It was at a small eatery three days into the trip that the direct route for their lives together was laid out. The eatery was next door to the hostel where they had stayed the night before. Jeff woke up early and went in to get something to snack on. He was the only one of those on the tour yet awake. Chloe sat at a table, looking over the day's itinerary and looking beautiful. Her dark hair was swept back from her face with a clip, and the combination of such concentration and beauty was irresistible to the men of the village. They began to circle her table, flirting boisterously without fear of derision. Jeff, like those men, was taken by her beauty as well, but flirted less obviously. He was concerned that she was attracting so much attention, but by the look on her face, he was certain she could handle the situation. She had probably handled similar situations all her life.

There were five men around her table. She did not look too flustered by them. A woman like her was used to such advances. But then the crowd began to grow. In fact, it doubled. Chloe could not see out of the group of swarthy Italians. Jeff could not see in through them. They were getting louder and their language more offensive. They were playfully yet forcefully tugging at one another and laughing, slapping backs and smearing words. Chloe was anxious and began to look around desperately for some escape.

It was then, as if offering a rope or a ladder, she saw Jeff extend his hand into the group. She took it, and he pulled her up and out, much to the contempt of the Italians.

"Thanks," she said. "I could have gotten out of that myself, you know."

"How would you have managed that?"

"I'm one hell of a climber."

DOWN THE WELL

CHLOE SOON regretted taking so much time off from work as well. The days were stretching out cold and silent, like cracks in the ice. The shadows of the night were the darkest she had ever known. And what few words Jeff had spoken to her did not amount to more than a paragraph. She walked through the cottage in a lonely self-embrace that was becoming a perpetual thing. The air of the cottage was chilled no matter how much wood was put in the fireplace. Jeff had chopped up the planks of wood left in the barn with more passion than she had seen from him in some time. Not all the wood stacked in the barn had rotted through, and it should have been enough to satisfy the small cottage. But the fire demanded more, licking each piece to ash with a deep, flamed tongue.

Chloe had gone into Wicker to curb her boredom but found nothing of interest there. The people were eerily pleasant, but she was just one of a number of faces in the quaint seaside community. The town seemed to have repopulated itself since she and Jeff had first come through. There was certainly more vigor to it, like it had awakened from a slumber. A few of the townsfolk asked her how she liked living in the cottage. None of them referred to Lana other than calling her "the old movie star" or "the actress." Behind their pleasant smiles, Chloe wondered if she saw the hint of mystery or even something more sinister. They were trying to figure her out.

"I could never live in a place like that," said Odette when she saw Chloe in her store again. Chloe guessed the quiet, larger-framed woman next to her was her sister, Alma. She stood back against a shelf of cigarettes with her hands folded in front of her as Odette chatted with Chloe at the register. Alma was a bloated replica of Odette, though she did not smile as much. She, it seemed, was for added atmosphere only. Not conversation.

Chloe regarded the sisters with curiosity. "Why not? What's wrong with the cottage?"

Alma shuffled ever so slightly behind Odette, and as if this was the cue to reel back in something cast too far, Odette said, "It… it's cold. It's so cold up on that hill."

And while that was the bitter truth, Chloe tossed the conversation around in her head after she left the store until it sounded more menacing than it had been. How would she know how cold the cottage was? And that shuffle Alma had done behind Odette…. What was that?

That was two days gone, and while Chloe was once again suffering the pangs of boredom, she did not care to head back into Wicker. At last, tired of waiting around the cottage for Jeff to say more than three words to her, Chloe put on her jacket and headed up the hill to the big house. Perhaps she could make friends with the old movie star.

"Wouldn't that be something to tell the grandkids?"

(The thought nearly stopped her in her tracks. One has to have children to have grandkids. And that was an impossibility. At least in biological terms. They could always adopt. Jeff's brother, Ethan, had adopted a baby, after all.)

The winds were fierce as she made her way past the trees and farther up the road. She tried to make out a face in every window of the big house or a silhouette up on the widow's walk, but there was never anything there. Chloe didn't suspect Lana was somewhere hidden behind a curtain and watching her come up the hill. Lana didn't seem the type to hide from individuals, despite her living situation hiding from society.

Chloe knocked, but there was no answer. The doorbell no longer worked. The porch creaked and moaned as she discreetly looked in the windows and called out for the actress. The rooms inside were dark, and she could barely see past the shadows. There were books in one of the rooms, though. She saw rows and stacks of large and cumbersome books. They looked too old to be of much use now. Who had time to turn pages when all one had to do was click Next on their reading device? Books were the leftover crumbs of a slower age.

The garden, overgrown yet still majestic, drew Chloe over from the porch. She walked beneath the old dead vines on the trellis and past the crumbling sculptures. Like the photographs she had found in the cottage, the garden looked ready to fade away completely. There were even tinges of the same browns and yellows. The paths were still apparent and in some use, though wild and weedy. There was a stone seat covered in a dried mossy cloak of some dead growth, directly across from a stone child angel. One of the wings had fallen from the sweet cherub and now lay on the ground at its feet. That had happened many years ago as evidenced by the density of the weeds and vines around it. Chloe sat down to study the angel more, but her eyes were drawn to the area just beside it. The angel was off center and not directly across from the seat as it should have been. It shared the bench sitter's attention with air.

Chloe stepped forward and brushed back the overgrowth beside the angel, beneath which was a creek stone. Not a word or design was written on it, yet it existed in its place for some reason. The wind howled around the house.

"That's Rebecca," came a voice from the path behind Chloe. "That's my daughter." It was a voice without emotion. Flat and trained.

Chloe stepped back from the stone at once, out of shock more than any sign of respect. "I'm sorry. I was coming up here to say hello. There was no answer at the door so I thought maybe…."

"I hardly ever come to the garden." The actress's eyes avoided the grave. They were focused on the visitor. "You must be very bored to come up here, all the way up here, against the wind."

"I've found that Jeff has filled his days with so much work that there's really nothing left for me to do at the cottage. He does the housework, everything. He must not trust me." It was meant in jest. Yet Chloe saw the slightest shade of sympathy for her on Lana's face.

"They find things to occupy their minds, don't they? Men, I mean. Things that are more easily controlled than a woman. More easily built… or destroyed." Lana had not moved. She belonged to this garden of death. She was its negligent caretaker.

"Jeff is a wonderful husband," Chloe asserted too quickly.

"I'm sure." But Chloe knew those eyes. They growled *Liar*.

Chloe pulled her jacket tight around her and began to move to the gates of the garden. Past them were long crooked stone stairs down a slope. "Well, I should be getting back to him. He'll be in need of something to eat, I suspect. I can at least do that."

Lana's shoulders fell just a little. "I would invite you in, but… not today. I'm not feeling at all myself today."

Chloe was suddenly very eager to be back at the cottage. The actress reminded her of that old photograph come to life, the one that had been swept over the cliff. Motionless, only without the frivolity. Chloe gave a gracious nod and a weak smile and then turned down the slope. Lana was back in the house before Chloe's feet had crossed the garden's threshold.

JEFF FELT his stomach flip, and the acid climbed up his throat, the thrill only an adventurer would know. Staring down the mouth of the well—its darkness strangely all too familiar—frightened and intrigued him at the same time. The creek stones changed from gray to black the farther down they went until Jeff wasn't sure if the well had a bottom at all, only more swallowing darkness. He didn't know how long he had been crouched on his knees looking into the hungry thing. By the sky, though, he knew it had been a while.

"How long has it been since you've had any water?" he said aloud. His voice whispered off the stones, bouncing down and away from him.

Uncovering the well was difficult. Jeff considered himself a strong man. He was the Golden Boy in his high school athletics department and would have done well in college if he had gone. But once the large stone had been pushed aside, the plank covering the mouth was of a particularly heavy wood, as if the stone had leaked its strength and petrified the slab. He struggled and grunted and yelled as he pushed the thing off. And then there was the odor that came from the rotten depths of the well. Jeff had to turn away momentarily so it could clear off.

Once the stone had been cleared, as he crouched there staring into the dark, he thought for certain Chloe would come rushing to the barn, summoned there by either his yelling or the wafting stench. He looked up and around for her, but she was not there. For a moment, he thought there was a figure, a small, thin form inside the barn, just beyond the door. But it was not Chloe's shape. Jeff wiped the sweat from his eyes and the figure was gone. His attention returned to the darkness below him.

A voice echoed in his head: What if she was here? What if Chloe was right beside you this minute? You could push her into the well. Would you have the courage to do that? You have the rage for it. Would you be able to channel all that rage you feel toward her into action? Could you forget about her? Just cover the well again and forget about that lying bitch? Or would you throw yourself in after her?

Jeff's fingers nearly dug into the stone as he peered over the well mouth. His grip on the edge of the well was tight to the point that it caused him pain. His knuckles were white, and he was shaking. The rage had never been as strong as this. His breathing had never been more labored.

Either way, it doesn't matter, does it? You'd be rid of her. Done with this act that was supposed to be a marriage. You could have been a good father to this stranger's baby. You could have had a family of your own after all.

You would have been a great father.

You wouldn't have needed her to be a great father. She could have died in labor and you could have raised the child on your own.

Jeff emerged from his ramblings like one waking from a dream. The thoughts clouded off and vanished. He stopped shaking, and his breathing returned to normal. He remained at the edge of the well a bit longer, peering into the familiar darkness. He wanted to see into it. To uncover more.

"I wonder," he said, his voice quaking a tiny bit. "I wonder what you've swallowed over the years. I wonder what's in your belly."

The wind knocked brittle branches against the old barn.

"These old wells always contain little treasures, don't they?" he asked as if someone was there with him, listening.

Jeff covered the well again, sliding the wood plank back in its original position but leaving the stone where he had pushed it. He didn't look to see if Chloe had returned from visiting the movie star yet. Instead, he jumped in the Jeep and raced down the hill toward town, making a mind's list of the things he would need or could use for his new project. There had to be a hardware store in the tiny community. And he was certain he had seen a few things at Odette and Alma's store that he could put to use. His heart raced with excitement, as if he were trying to outrun someone. Someone who would stop him and say "No. You can't do that" like he was a child. Like he was a sick child with no free will of his own.

Once down Bad Luck Hill and onto the creek bed, he began to feel calmer. The Jeep was another matter. It stalled on the rocks in the middle of the stream. Jeff did not immediately attempt to fix the problem. He stared for a moment to his left, as far down the creek bed as he could see, before it mildly turned at a bend. A blast of wind rocked the Jeep. The wind around this place had curious strength and personality. It was almost abusive in sound and touch. It cursed and smacked. Jeff turned the key and the Jeep started at once.

Jeff was right about the store he and Chloe had visited on their first trip into Wicker. He found plenty he could use there, as if they were stocking the place just for him. After patrolling the aisles, throwing anything that might be useful for his descent down the well into a wobbly shopping cart, Jeff approached the register. Odette sat there expectantly. She was dressed nicely, but in a casual manner, and smiled pleasantly. It was an expression she probably always wore, given the main revenue for any place of business in Wicker was most likely tourism. That same pleasant smile was hammered onto every child's face in Wicker on their first day of kindergarten. "Must be nice to tourists."

"Fixing up the old place?" she asked.

"Yes. Just doing a little work. Keeping busy." He placed a coil of rope on the counter.

"Your wife was in here the other day. Such a dear, pretty thing. She met my sister, Alma. You just missed her."

"Who?"

"My sister, Alma. You just missed her."

"I'm sure we'll meet eventually. I imagine in towns like this, there are eyes everywhere. I imagine I won't be able to go anywhere without it being reported to someone. Your sister Alma will know exactly where I am all the time if she ever wants to meet me. I imagine I'm being watched very closely."

"Quite an imagination. But you're not wrong." She rung the items up nonchalantly. "I say, you're not wrong."

"Suspicious townsfolk here?"

She stopped what she was doing and looked at him as if he had missed her point completely. "Sure."

Jeff found the sudden quaking in his knees to be most annoying. The symptoms of the disease his father had passed down to him could be confused with fear. Still, this woman did make him nervous. Beneath her pleasantness lay… what?

"Do you like the little place?" She had swiped Jeff's credit card and held it out to him between two thin, pruned fingers.

"Should I not?"

She shook her head. Some of her smile dropped off. "I suppose as long as you know what you're doing, as long as you know your future or the history of where you're at, things will be just fine. But I should tell you—"

From somewhere behind Odette, in a back room, there was a loud banging. It shook the wall. Odette looked over her shoulder. Her eyes jittered. "That's Alma," she said. "I should go see what she wants."

Jeff headed out to the Jeep with his implements of distraction. Odette had put him off. She reminded him of Chloe. That look in Chloe's eyes whenever she had one of her "feelings" was reminiscent of the look he had just seen from Odette. Jeff couldn't get Chloe to take a step if she had a "feeling." Psychic bullshit was what he called these excuses. She used to have them a lot, but not so much anymore. At least, none that he knew of. But then, lately he avoided her glances. Maybe she had them more than he knew.

He looked into the bag as he lifted it onto the backseat of the Jeep. The cable wires were on top of the rope, and there were all the Internet trappings as well. He'd get the computer hooked up to the Internet so that Chloe would leave him in peace. He would need lots of time to himself if he was going to literally and figuratively get to the bottom of that well. Chloe had a lot of Internet friends, both psychic and otherwise. Let her alone with them. She could have an online affair for all he cared.

CHLOE DID not stay on the gravel road as she walked home from the big house. She made a detour through the woods. At least there, shielded by the trees, Lana could not watch her through the telescope on the widow's walk. The afternoon sky was still a bright gray, and the wind bellowed through the forest, sometimes threatening to bring down a tree. She had no desire to head directly back to the cottage.

"What have I gotten myself into?" she said aloud.

Once again, everything she said was met with silence. It surrounded her, muffled her ears like the wind or like water to a drowning person.

She walked for a while, uncertain if she was going in circles or if she had even turned once. Her attention was elsewhere, on Jeff and the cottage and her mother and father. On problems she could not fix because they were formless. But at least an hour had passed. At least. She shook her head at her own stupidity.

"Pay attention!" Those were the first words she told anyone who went on her tours. "Pay attention to your surroundings at all times. Watch for signs in case you get lost. There are always signs."

Now she stood in the middle of a strange wood and had no idea in which direction to go to find the cottage. She turned, listening for the sea. The trees cracked and popped around her. She knew the right thing to do would be to stay put and let Jeff find her. But when would that be? And if he had to come looking for her, she knew he would be irritable about it. She took off in the direction of the sound of the sea.

As she walked farther, she heard notes. Music through the trees, very quick and sharp. She could not pass it off as a trick of the ears because she recognized it. It was the fiddle she had heard, usually on the edges of sleep. She kept walking. Her heart jumped every time a note was played. They were sporadic and uneven and not truly a melody, as if she was hearing random notes through the static of a radio. She focused on what was in front of her and walked faster, trying to keep her head down so she wouldn't see.

The tip of her shoe hit something hard that was hidden by inches of leaves, and she nearly lost her balance. She danced forward before she steadied herself and then turned to investigate what she had tripped over. She then stepped on another such thing directly in front of her. They were stones, a small garden of them. Wiping away the leaves and debris that had covered and caked one of the small creek stones, she made out barely legible, but deeply carved writing:

PLUCKY

It was a pet cemetery. Chloe smiled. "Very sweet," she whispered.

Then she heard the notes again. The fiddling. But it was louder now. Closer. And she could hear the song, a frenzied piece that gave her goose bumps. And it was right in front of her.

"Don't see!" she whispered to herself. "Don't see it!"

She stood and backed away. There was the image of a man playing a fiddle as passionately, as furiously and dangerously as Chloe had ever seen anything done. He cut into the strings with his bow. His frothing mouth was a twisted distortion; his hair, a greasy mess; his clothes, torn and ragged. He stopped suddenly and looked at her with eyes ringed and unwrung. The whites had eaten all the color from them. With his bow, he motioned for the stone she had first tripped over. She could do nothing but run.

The branches seemed to attack her as she raced through the woods, trying to find an out. Any out.

What have you gotten yourself into? What the hell was that? What have you gotten yourself into? Oh God, help me!

The fiddling followed her, but only briefly. It faded as the woods cleared and Chloe saw the little red barn ahead of her. She slammed into the back side of the structure and kept her hands to it until she was around the front and, to her relief, could see the cottage. Jeff had just pulled up in the Jeep and was getting an assortment of bagged items out of the backseat.

Chloe collected herself. She had to tell Jeff about her new "feelings." He had to know. This was dangerous. They were in danger.

Jeff saw her and stopped, his arms loaded.

"What's wrong with you?" he asked. Everything he said these days sounded accusatory.

"Nothing. I mean… I was just going for a run. Jeff, I saw something that—"

"Through the woods? A run? In those clothes? Doubtful."

That tone. That tone made her blood boil. Maybe this wasn't the right time to tell him. Maybe she could wait until later. "What did you get in town?"

"Things. Stuff. We're going to get you hooked up to the Internet."

ANYONE BRAVE enough to weather the winds of Bad Luck Hill late at night might, on certain evenings, chance upon quite a sight in the big house's garden. Anyone daring to get that close might well deserve the rights to tell the story of what they saw. And if the moon were just right, what a show!

Anyone watching would see a woman shedding her garments as she danced around a one-winged angel. They would see her arms gesture in artistic echoes of a dance. Something unchoreographed, but beautiful just the same. When her last piece of clothing would fall to the ground, it would be with elegance, not shame. Anyone watching would see her touch the angel's face, cradling it tenderly. They might even hear her low humming of a private melody, though it was doubtful her voice would carry above the winds.

They would not know of the henbane, the mandrake, or the deadly nightshade she used alternately. They could not see the face of the angel distort to become that of a little girl or an angry man, then change again to something altogether demonic and damning. They could not know this was why she would suddenly collapse and cower in fear before the statue, completely naked, and cry "I didn't do it! I didn't do it!" until sleep took her. They could not know, nor would they care, that her heart broke every evening. No. They would not be able to see this. And things unseen matter very little to those but the seer.

ETHAN

THANK GOD for the Internet, that invisible savior of the bored and lonely, of the sleepless and lost. The invention that had kept Chloe company on many nights this past year proved its worth yet again while Jeff slept behind the closed door of the bedroom.

Chloe was wrapped in her favorite blanket with a cup of hot tea steaming on the kitchen table beside the laptop as she net-searched and occasionally chatted with faceless friends. She needed those friends on nights like this. She missed them, especially now that she lived in so remote a place. Here, not even turning on every light in the cottage could hush the shadows. Whether it was the wind or not, the night noises of the little place scared her awake, making her insomnia even worse. But she had not heard the fiddler this night. Thank God for that. She trembled at the thought of him—the white eyes, the haggard face, and the emotionless invitation with the bow. She dared not look out the windows. There were dark forms against the night out there, maybe worse than the fiddler. Shadows and silhouettes that could not be seen in the daylight. They were watching. She could feel them as she had felt them on the drive up the hill that first day. Things she could not see. There were things she could not see all around her: her friends on the Internet, the forms in the dark, Jeff's love….

Jeff's love was so invisible, so barely there as to be nonexistent, maybe the one true myth of all the invisible things. As she wandered the Internet, she found herself pressing each key with extra force whenever she thought of Jeff. Every Backspace was hit more emphatically than the last. Every Control, every Shift, every Escape was an angry plea. He had made her hate herself so, and that instilled in her a rage toward him that was only seen in the loneliest hours—another invisible thing.

She had tried to embrace him once in bed. That was a few months after he had relented and agreed to try and save their marriage. He shrugged the embrace off, though. Truthfully, Chloe knew the marriage was already past saving, but what else had she to cling to? He was the physical manifestation of all her life's mistakes now. His disappointment in her was her own.

The boring white light of the web page she had wandered upon was interrupted momentarily by a little box that popped up in the corner of the screen. Ethan had signed on. He most likely saw that she was on the messenger as well, though he would never invite her to chat. They never messaged one another but kept each other on their contact lists just the same. With the Internet, there was the luxury of only being seen or heard when one wanted. Unlike real conversations, a person could avoid an awkward pause on the Internet without seeming rude. Jeff and Ethan were masters at avoiding each other now, both in the real world and the cyber world. Ethan had been out of Jeff's life for nearly two years. That was something Chloe thought was for the best. She sighed and pulled her blanket more tightly around her.

She remembered when Ethan had called and told them about the adoption he and his husband, Kelton, were going through. How they needed Jeff to speak for Ethan's personal character at some type of hearing. She remembered how the thought of a man having a husband and those two husbands adopting a child had disturbed her.

"I'm so happy for you," Chloe had said even as she felt a tug somewhere deep inside. A feeling. Something dreadful, something deadly, yet somehow different than her other "feelings."

She and Jeff were on their way to the hearing when Chloe couldn't keep quiet any longer. Every day since Ethan's call, the feeling had gotten stronger. At the halfway point on the drive, it was screaming in her head. They were getting closer and closer to something she could not place and yet threatened her with promised poison. It wasn't the fact that Jeff was going to speak on behalf of two gay men to adopt. It was something more akin to a warning of ensuing danger. When they stopped at a gas station, she finally told Jeff that she, at least, could go no farther.

"My brother needs me," he said in between boxes of cereal and bags of potato chips.

But she pleaded with him. Her shaking had worsened, and he held her tight to calm her as those in the store stared. That was when Jeff had loved her. That was when he would do anything for her. He led her back to the car and they headed home. It wasn't until later that night that they heard the Buskeaton Bridge, which was on their route to Ethan, had fallen, causing the deaths of twenty-three people. Jeff gave her a strange look when he heard.

"I didn't cause this," she said, curled up on the couch. "Did I? I didn't cause this?"

Now she sat at the kitchen table and posed the same question for a different circumstance to the empty room. Her own voice brought her back. She looked around, grasping for light, but avoiding the windows. Never look out the windows.

Beside the keyboard lay the group of photos she had found days earlier minus the one that had been whipped out of her grip and over the cliff by the wind. She wondered where it would eventually end up. Where would the wind take that photo? The photograph that caught her eye now was of a little girl in the very room they called their bedroom. She was alone in the black and white photo, staring at the camera in an annoyed manner as if it were disturbing some important conversation she was involved in. Indeed, she sat on the floor, toy dinner place settings for her and an invisible guest.

And yet not invisible.

As Chloe focused more intently on the photograph, she noticed a definite outline of something just across from the child.

Like a dark sliver of moon floating just above the other place setting. And under it, written on the photo in a child's scrawl, was the nearly completely faded word rascal.

Chloe stared for a moment, wiping at the scrawl with her thumb. She leaned over the keyboard intently. She needed more information. What could she type into the Internet—that modern oracle—to find out more about this little cottage? What set of words would bring back to her the information she wanted? All the answers in the world were out there to any question ever asked, but they were all invisible unless one knew how to call to them.

The house creaked, and from its walls and the kitchen floor came a sound like a low moan. So low that Chloe hardly recognized it at first. Then the silence of the cottage slinked away and let the moan grow. She could not explain it away as "the noises an old house makes." She could not explain it at all. She clutched tighter at herself in the blanket and began to shake, not daring to look away from the screen, feeling the moan crowd around her and up from the floorboards, both heartbreaking and heart-stopping. She covered her ears to drown out the sound and wish away the fiddler before he even began. She wanted to cry out for Jeff.

The computer screen turned black, and all the lights around her first flickered, then expired completely. The moan continued to grow until she could not take it anymore. She flung the blanket from her shoulders and raced to the bedroom. The moan followed her, echoing off the walls and mingling with her own cries like a wild nightmare.

She fell into the bed with a piercing scream. At once, Jeff woke up, sitting and staring at her in frightened anticipation. "What? What is it?"

She was shaken by the utter silence around her now. The lights were on again as if nothing had happened. But she knew something had happened. The thunder of her heart was proof of that.

"What's wrong, Chloe?" Jeff repeated. He did not reach out for her to comfort her.

Nothing. There was nothing she could say to him. She was too aware of this place. He was too accepting of it.

He dropped back to the pillow, shaking his heavy head in irritation.

ETHAN SAW Chloe's name and icon pop onto the computer screen. It took him aback. Her cartoon icon resembled her to such a degree that it was like coming face to face with her. Ethan's sense of unease was growing. His skin had been crawling for the last hour, and he couldn't help but think it had something to do with his brother, Jeff, though he hadn't the vaguest idea why.

Kelton was asleep. He had been up most of the night before taking care of their son, Malcolm, so he had gone to bed early tonight. They called Malcolm "Bug" because, as Kelton had once said, "He's as cute as a bug." Bug had been ill for the past few days and only now was sleeping soundly. Kelton was the one who usually took care of things. He had always been the more maternal one. Ethan was so busy with work.

"You need to spend more time with Bug," Kelton had said on numerous occasions. "He's growing up fast and you're going to regret not being around."

"I have to work, Kel," Ethan would say. "I don't have the luxury of working from home like you. Things will settle down soon. I promise. Then the three of us will have plenty of time together."

"You promise?"

"I promise, baby."

Ethan had volunteered to look after Bug tonight so Kelton could rest. He had just spent an hour getting Bug back to sleep after an illness-induced nightmare. Those were the worst, and Ethan knew it from experience. When he and Jeff were younger,

Jeff got sick quite often. His nightmares would set him to screaming. Ethan often wouldn't sleep at all, waiting for Jeff to scream and their parents to go rushing into Jeff's room to care for him. Ethan envied the attention given to Jeff. He envied the sound of his parents' running feet as they made their way past his own room and to Jeff's. Everything was always about Jeff. He was the Golden Boy.

Now where was Jeff? Hours away, and Ethan suspected he was quite happy there with Chloe. Ethan's anger had subsided over what had happened between them. The adoption had gone fine, after all. But the fact that Jeff didn't show up and all Ethan got was a phone call telling him that Chloe didn't "feel right" put him at a loss for words. That was, until he got back home and raged his indignation to Kelton's sympathetic ear.

Still, despite what had happened and the two years that had passed, something in Ethan's gut told him to get in contact with Jeff. The darkness of the study around him pressed him to do so. Chloe was, after all, right there for the asking. It was that simple. He only had to say "How's Jeff?"

His mind drifted, though, to his parents. To his father and his mother arguing from one end of the house to the other. They had argued all the time. The house was on edge constantly, though it hadn't always been that way. There was peace once, but that was before his father was told he had a tumor, something dreadful and genetic that was easily passed from generation to generation. Something that could not be tested for until later in life when it was all but too late. One did not need a degree in psychiatry to see that their mother had blamed their father for possibly passing the disorder down to one of her sons. Possibly even the favorite one. There was a current of raging animosity for years. The house was thick with it. Even Ethan felt the brunt of its force once or twice when he would catch his father or mother watching him, he knew they were thinking, "Why not him instead of our precious Jeffrey?"

The boys could not see the illness in their father. The man looked as solid as he ever had. "Any illness worth its salt knows to stay hidden," he'd said. "It's like oxygen or love, but mean and angry."

Like oxygen or love… or guilt.

Ethan was tested for the disease when he was older and on his own. The disease had skipped him. He supposed it had skipped Jeff as well or else his brother surely would have told him. But that good news came too late for the family. Their father, years earlier, had killed himself, running the car he was driving into an old oak tree while returning from a dinner date. Their mother was in the passenger seat and she survived. She was still in a coma at a hospital a few miles from where Ethan now lived with Kelton and Bug. Though Jeff had at the time of the accident just become of the age to legally care for Ethan, who was but two years younger, he decided not to do so. He did not even tell his brother of this decision, but instead one day just left. Ethan spent the next two years in state care, visiting his comatose mother often. When Jeff finally did return, he brought Chloe with him. Her face went white when Ethan introduced Kelton, whom he had met while in state care, as his husband.

Mother's face was blank now. Her pain was gone or, God forbid, hiding beneath a pale shroud. But it was best for him not to think of such morbid things. If he did, if he allowed himself to focus on what waited in the dark, he might never recover. To Ethan, a blank stare was more terrifying than the most horrific grimace of pain. Ethan had stopped being afraid of the dark soon after the accident. He stopped seeing imaginary nightmares, because there was a real one just down the street at a care facility, and it had his mother's face.

Ethan clicked on Chloe's icon, but as he did so, her name disappeared from the screen. She had signed off or—and this he found more likely—was simply refusing to talk with him.

He soon signed off as well. He needed to check on Bug anyway. He'd give Jeff a call tomorrow if he could find the new cell phone number. Wading through discomfort in the daylight was always preferable to doing it in the stillness of night.

THE BRIDGE

STANDING ON the small stone stoop outside the kitchen door, Chloe watched the barn. Her arms were folded yet again, as much from a pensive attitude as from a chill. Her brow was pinched in deliberation. The move hadn't helped at all, and she now accepted that it was ridiculous to have thought it ever would have. They could live on this hill above the rest of the world for ages and not see another soul (but for crazy old Lana Pruitt), and still Jeff would never see Chloe the same way he once had. And, in truth, she would never see him the same either. Gone was the gorgeous man with the warm smile who gave her inappropriate hugs at company meetings as her mother looked on. She'd never feel those arms again in that way. She'd never again feel the warm crush of his body on hers while making love. Past mistakes, she found, anchored their pain to the present. It never lessened, and never had the chance to slip away to the horizon where it might possibly disappear forever.

But there was nothing for it. She had to live with him now that they had bought the cottage. And he had to live with her. She would make an effort. Maybe something could be salvaged, even if it was just a shadow or an act. Chloe decided that, like Lana, she could learn to act.

She entered the open doorway of the old barn with some trepidation. This was Jeff's space and she felt like an invader. Her arms were still crossed, and she massaged her elbows. She stood in the door space for a moment. The light from the gray sky came through the wood walls and ceiling of the barn like some divine light. It had the feel of something spiritual. Of a cathedral. But it was not at all comforting, just overbearing and ready to crush her with accusations.

She found Jeff on the muddy floor of the barn behind a reassembled stack of rotten firewood. He was tightening a bright yellow rope. It trailed out the barn door to the well. Beside him, more rope snaked and coiled. He seemed to be constructing some kind of pulley system using the barn as tethering. The firewood served as uneven shelves for Jeff's mountain climbing gear. Jeff had the skill for climbing mountains. He had done it many times with the company, leading tours. Chloe had done fewer of those type of tours. The altitude did not appeal to her. She could lead tours through the lower hills of a range, but nothing that involved crampons or ice picks.

She looked out toward the well as she leaned against the barn. "So, that's the well," she said, her voice weak and wary. "Are you going to descend? To see what's down there?"

Jeff looked up at her. His face was smeared with black mud, one especially thick wipe across the left cheek. He studied her momentarily. His fingers stopped working the rope. Chloe realized he wasn't studying her, he was judging her. She suddenly felt very bare—naked, but in such a way she had never been before. Vulnerable and stripped of even her skin.

"What do you want?" Jeff said. His voice was deep and angry. The whites of his eyes glowed in the relative darkness of the barn. If he were frothing at the mouth, he could not have seemed more vicious.

"I just came out to—" But she was stopped short, her attention grabbed by a new, disturbing air. At first, she thought it was her own stammering, but there was an unmatched quality to this sound. It was a giggle—menacing, but a giggle still, and it came from nowhere that she could see.

She looked at her husband, suddenly on alert. "Did you hear that?"

"What do you want?" he repeated. His stare had not changed. He dug his fingers into his forearm, scratching ferociously. Chloe noticed his skin was now raw in that spot, as if he had a rash or bug bite there and had been scratching for a while.

"I just wanted to see what you were up to," she said. She began edging away. She had never feared Jeff before, but this.... This hardly seemed like Jeff. She felt like a cornered animal. As she moved off, Jeff returned his attention to the rope.

Chloe walked, chilled and frightened, back to the cottage. She kept her eyes on the ground. She would wait until she got inside the cottage before she'd allow a single tear to fall. But there would be tears. It was over. It was all over. Their marriage. Their friendship. Everything. There was nothing left to pick over.

JEFF WAS immersed. He did not have time for Chloe's cloying attempts to regain her footing in his life. He had a project to work on, and it had begun to swallow large swaths of his time. He could not resist the well. He had to know what lay far below in the darkness.

He tightened and untightened the same length of rope again and again, not realizing what he was doing. The feel of the rope, the sense of purpose, put him at ease and took him out of his unsatisfactory life. The barn and the well had become his sanctuary.

He had been dreaming so vividly of late. Even while working on the well, he would find himself lost in the dreams. There was a boy, around twelve or thirteen judging by his height, but Jeff never saw his face. He was always seen from behind. The first Jeff had seen of him, the boy sat near naked on the ground in the woods wearing a pair of dirty underwear and a large-brimmed brown hat. Perhaps too large for his pointed head. The boy had something in his lap and was working furiously on it. Feverishly and unnaturally fast. Around him lay the bloody carcasses of small animals: birds, rabbits, and moles.

The boy turned quickly, as if being called, and then got up and ran. He ran to the big house on the hill. The sky was mute and heavy over the structure. The boy stopped suddenly in the yard and tensed. He backed off slowly, and the big house began to transform. From wood and stone, it became flesh and bone. The widow's walk became a woman's head, and it looked disapprovingly down at the boy. Its roof had become her messy dark hair, and the railing was a line of her sharp teeth. The boy screamed and he began to run back to the cottage. He ran as fast as he could, but she caught him with her arms made of the splintered porch.

At once, the boy was in the barn, being whipped by the woman, who now stood all too human before him. Jeff tried to intervene, but the woman would not allow it. She continued to thrash at the boy without mercy with a finely whittled tree branch, leaving deep red marks on the boy's bare legs and arms. He howled in pain and rage, his face still a blur to Jeff.

"He gets what he gets because he sins," the woman said as she continued whipping the boy. "You must stop it before it begins."

Then she let go of the branch and it became a rope. It wrapped itself around the boy, tying him to one of the beams in the barn. Again, Jeff made a move to interfere.

The woman flung him back. "It gets what it gets because it sins!" she screamed.

From the woman's push, Jeff fell back to the mouth of the well and peered down into it.

The woman stood at the barn door. "Well, you fell and found the well. It will tell, oh it will tell! A gateway, an opening, out of some hell."

The darkness of the well enveloped him, and he woke. And when Jeff awoke from such dreams and visions, they did not fill him with dread. No. It was excitement that filled him, for he knew then that there was adventure yet to be had.

THE ACTRESS saw everything from her widow's walk. She saw the ocean mock the sky. She saw the sky rage at the water. At night, she saw the lights from across the bay, tiny and twinkling. She saw the change in weather before it arrived. And through the telescope, she now saw Chloe, the new cottage owner, trudging up the hill.

Lana didn't think Chloe was headed for the big house. Truthfully, Chloe didn't look to be headed anywhere. She was just walking, climbing up the hill and tiring herself out. Her arms were wrapped around her body, and Lana sensed the loss the girl was feeling. Loss was like a bridge and tackle. Anyone who has known it—true loss, not just the displacement of a favorite trinket—anyone who has honestly known it connects automatically, almost angrily and with a starving need, to those souls who are similar. The actress felt Chloe was throwing her tackle. The question was, could Lana accept it? Would she want to? She'd been alone so long, everything else was foreign now. To seek comfort in another human being would be... immoral.

As Chloe walked closer, Lana found that she wished Chloe might look up to the widow's walk. To connect, if just a little.

"Here I am," she whispered. But they were words not meant to be heard. They were at once taken by the same mad breeze that chafed her face raw. Words dead from their first utterance.

Opening up to Chloe would be selfish, Lana chided herself. The actress had laid her bed with self-accusations, and she had to sleep in it. The wind agreed. A friend would not help matters anyway. Lana felt she was already hurtling toward the end of the scene, her lines flubbed or the script rewritten.

Her husband, Michael, had asked her not to take the role in the film. Her last role. A diabolical mother with dialogue that stretched into the absurd and the campy. He had begged her to spend more time with their daughter, Rebecca.

"You have one chance to be a good mother," he had pleaded with her. "You'll have other film sets to go to. Please stay!"

He was so desperate that she not go that she almost relented. But Lana assured him there would be plenty of time once she returned from the shoot. Just this last shoot and then she'd take some time off. That seemed to satisfy him. The last Lana saw of her daughter was the girl's teary-eyed good-bye. She and her father waved from the widow's walk as Lana was whisked away in the long black car down the hill.

The film would flop, though she received decent marks for it. Lana's last desperate effort to revive her career failed. She was a glittering has-been. Not even the tragedy that followed could raise the public's interest in the actress.

Michael had called her on the set continuously on the last few days of shooting. He was even more bothersome than usual with the frequency of his calls. She began to avoid them.

"Tell him I have a scene," she told her assistant. "Tell him I'm busy."

Finally, on the last day of shooting, he was calling every couple of minutes. It exasperated her.

"What is it, Michael? I'll be home in a day! Can't it wait?"

She came home to find Michael standing over a fresh patch of dirt in the garden. His eyes were red from crying and fatigue. They would have a private memorial service for Rebecca there. He never looked at Lana again. At least not in the eye. She was grateful for that mercy. She could not look into his either. She was fearful of the things she would see.

Chloe waved from below. She had caught the actress in the midst of her own sorrow.

A bridge.

Lana reluctantly waved back but did not smile. That would be the toll for the bridge. Leave your smile before you cross.

And somewhere inside her, that voice that laid her bed with guilt said: Invite her in. This is it, Lana. It begins. This all leads up to your glorious final scene. There will be a brilliant score. There will be weeping in the audience. And then you will die, because you have to die. You've seen enough films. You've been in enough of them too. It's the scene any actress would give their right arm to perform.

WHAT'S PAST

AT THE kitchen window, Chloe mixed the sugar in the tea and watched Jeff swing the axe into the half-rotted block of wood. She wasn't trying any longer. She didn't expect the iced tea to make her husband suddenly swim out of his angry tide. She was making him tea so she would have something to do. That was all.

The day before, she had been invited into the big house by Lana. It was a strange visit, as expected. The actress was on her widow's walk and waved down to her, then motioned Chloe inside. Lana seemed a specter or a spirit dressed in her dark clothes at the top of the house. It was not a welcoming look, but Chloe went in just the same.

They drank tea in the library, a room so packed with thick books there was barely space for furniture. In fact, what books weren't being used for literary purposes were piled upon one another as footrests or tables. The smell of slowly decaying pages—a strangely comforting thing—permeated the air. Almost a smoke, so heavy was its odor.

Not much was said between the two women, and what words that were spoken did not have any earth-shattering importance. They were simply directions and strained pleasantries: "Have a seat," "Would you like some sugar," etc. Every sentence and its response was bookended by an awkward silence. Awkward for Chloe, that was. The actress didn't seem to mind the stoic moments. Chloe looked over old tattered volumes of literature and photo albums during those pauses. The pictures in the albums told Chloe more than any words ever could about the faded star.

There was an actress.

She was married to a handsome man.

They had a daughter.

They had been happy.

Now the actress was alone in the big house.

She was unhappy.

The end.

Chloe wondered if, in getting to know Lana, she might ever fill in what had happened in the time between "they had been happy" and "the end." Lana seemed to watch Chloe's expressions as she looked over the photos. Chloe felt the hard stare. She made a slight connection between the photo album and a book of the occult in Lana's collection. It held a place of esteem in the room, the only book opened on a table and seemingly in constant use. The table was cleared of all else but a couple of candles.

Desperate wanting, Chloe knew, would cause people to try anything. Anything at all. Desperate wanting could cause people to believe in the invisible with more zeal than what was right in front of their eyes.

The axe struck the wood with a harsh knock. Chloe watched it rise and fall as she brought the iced tea to Jeff. Jeff had found the axe in the barn. The blade no longer gleamed. It was too old and dull for that. Now it bit into the wood, snarling and rusting, instead of splitting it. To split a block, even a rotting one, took more than a few swings. Yet it still looked dangerous to Chloe. An implement of chaos.

They needed the wood for this winter. Just this one. They planned to get a gas stove after this year. Or that was the plan once things between them had smoothed over and their marriage was healed. Since that would never happen, though, there was no use spending the money. They'd be gone by spring. She would at least. Jeff might choose to stay.

The axe scattered the block of wood into pieces at last. One of the larger, more jagged bits landed at her feet.

"Don't stand too close to me," Jeff said under heavy breaths. "Not when I do this. You could get hurt." He took the tea from her. "Thank you."

"I thought you could use a drink." The hope in her voice was gone, as was the pleading. She was disgusted with herself for clinging so long to it.

As he drank, he rested an elbow on the axe hilt. The blade pressed into the ground. Wood splinters surrounded him. How easy would it be for the love of her life to sink the dull axe blade into her skull? Would she die instantly, or would there need to be excessive hacking, blow after blow? "Hold on, dear, while I cut off your head. Stop dancing around the yard, dear. Stop dancing."

There it was again. A giggling, as if it had heard Chloe's thoughts. It came from the barn door this time. Jeff seemed not to notice. He kept drinking and avoiding her eyes. Still, that avoidance was better than the vengeful stare she had received from him when he was fixing the rope in the barn. And this time, she was positive the voice wasn't in her head. It couldn't be. She wanted to ask if Jeff had heard it but knew better. Jeff hated her "feelings," her sensing of things. Even if it had saved his life once before.

He took a final drink from the glass of tea and handed it back to Chloe. She noticed the welts and scratches on his forearms and now a couple on his neck.

"I must have gotten into some ivy or something," he said.

Chloe didn't pursue the matter, though her doubts were multitude. "I'm going to head into town," she said, "maybe check out the library. I need something to read. I'll pick up some cream for you. You wouldn't want that to get infected."

Jeff said nothing. He picked up the axe and waited for Chloe to walk away, holding it with both hands while he stared down a new block of wood.

She put the glass on the kitchen counter and left, a breaking of wood coinciding with the slam of the Jeep door. She had questions. She needed answers. And there were only two places to find them: the town and the actress. She'd try the town first.

THE TOWN library was a boxy place set apart from the other buildings and given a special place on a small hill. It was as historic as the rest of Wicker, though not particularly beautiful. The only thing of interest about the architecture of the structure was the little dome that bubbled up out of its center. The library reminded Chloe of a contestant's buzzer on a game show, ready to be slammed in answer to some trivia question about film or history. Little towns are cute. They think cute things. They strut their cuteness along rivers and immaculate main streets. They do this so their secrets and acidic malevolence can be better hidden.

Chloe still felt the eyes of the town on her. There was perhaps nothing malevolent about the township's gaze toward her in particular, but there was a difference in how she and Jeff were seen by Wicker (as its newest residents) and how the average tourist was seen. At some point, she surmised, the town would have to decide whether or not to let her in on all of their little secrets. In the meantime, they just smiled pleasantly.

The history of the town and the surrounding county was public record, but Chloe found very little about the hill on which she and Jeff lived. The census, while going back many years, offered her only a small amount of information other than the surnames of the land owners. The only mention Chloe could find about the hill itself in the archives was when Lana Pruitt had moved there years earlier:

FAMOUS ACTRESS MOVES TO BAD LUCK HILL

Bad Luck Hill. She wasn't certain it was the proper name of the place. There wasn't anything to confirm or dismiss it as such. But Chloe acknowledged that, from her experience there so far, it was an appropriate sobriquet. As far as where that particular nickname had come from, again, there was no clue. At last, she sat back in her chair and breathed deeply in frustration, disappointed her search had turned up nothing.

Her attention was caught up and drawn to the window as a small stream, a parade, of people dressed in black took to the street. They passed the library, not a smile among them. Eight tall and thin pallbearers carried a casket at the front of the mourners, and leading them all was the quiet sister Chloe had seen at the store named Alma. Other townsfolk watched the parade from the sidewalks, stopping in shows of respect.

The town librarian, a Mr. Craft, balding, with deep-set eyes and an old voice, came up beside her. "It's a sad day," he said.

"Was it someone very important?" Chloe asked.

"Odette? Yes. Very important. I haven't seen a turnout like this since the herring run. But at least the poor thing died in her sleep. That's all we can ask for, isn't it? That's all any of us can ask for."

"I suppose so." She was reminded to get the cream for Jeff's rash. But would the store even be open now?

"Did you find what you were looking for?" the librarian asked as she readied to leave. She had been watched. It was a disconcerting feeling that was becoming all too familiar here and something she realized she would need to get used to.

"Not really," she said, slipping back into her jacket.

Mr. Craft had a mortuary look about him—tall and thin, with long fingers that could easily navigate delicate situations. His head, like the rest of him, was narrow, as if pressed.

"I was looking for information on my new home," Chloe said. "Just as a project. But there doesn't seem to be anything here about the cottage, or even the hill, that can help me."

"There was a fire here a few years ago that wiped out nearly all the older books and archives." He looked very interested in her project. It was as if his eyes came forward from their deep-set positions in his head. He wore a slight grin that made him appear like a wilting jack-o'-lantern. "My cousin, Mary Beth, is the town archivist. She comes in once a week if you'd like to meet with her. I'm sure she'd be happy to help you with your research. Our family has run the library since Wicker was founded. We have records that haven't been shelved here for decades. I'm sure there's something in there about Bad Luck Hill. In fact, I'm positive there is."

"Um… maybe. It's not that important." She made an awkward attempt to leave. Mr. Craft's curiosity for her project seemed intrusive.

The librarian stepped in front of her with one long stride. "I can help," he said enthusiastically, his words stretching like snakes on a vine. "I can answer any questions you might have. Or, at least, help spread some rumors." He smiled with all the charm his slender form allowed. The edges of his smile seemed to lift the rest of his body like a hanger.

Chloe understood she was not going to be let out of the building until she let him talk. "Okay. Why is it called Bad Luck Hill?"

"Oh, that's nothing. Just silly teenagers and their ghost stories. That's not to say there hasn't been…."

"Go on."

Mr. Craft looked over his shoulders, yet barely turned his head. There was no one else in the library, but he appeared cautious just the same. "It's all quite entertaining," he said enthusiastically. "The hill itself is nothing more than haunt legends. But the big house and your cottage"—he pointed a long, untrimmed finger at her—"those are the real stories. I shouldn't be telling you any of this, really."

"Why not?"

He raised his index finger as if to hush her. "Before the actress bought the place—long before—a family lived in that little cottage below it… your cottage. A mother, a father, and three tykes, if you can believe it, all cramped into that itty-bitty cottage. Can you imagine children? In there?"

"No."

"No, indeed. Well, apparently, from eyewitnesses"—the librarian drew closer to Chloe—"apparently, the oldest boy was quite disturbed. He started with animals. He'd kill them, skin them. You know, the sort of thing that might someday manifest itself into a serial killer. That's what they say on the television, anyway. That's how they say serial killers start out. Well, his parents didn't know what to do. Thank goodness they didn't come into town too often with the children. Nobody wants to be around a future serial killer, after all.

"From what I've been told—I was just a baby when all this happened, mind you—from what I've been told, the father died of something. Most likely from the stress brought on by having a lunatic son. One couldn't then expect the mother to raise three children well, especially if one of them was…." He twirled his eyes and let his strip of a tongue hang from his mouth. "The mother decided to lock the boy in the barn like he was some animal. I guess it was all she could do. After all, she couldn't have him snapping one day and harming the other children… or anyone here in town, for that matter…."

"None of the eyewitnesses reported that the boy was living in the barn?"

"Living?" He smiled crookedly. "Nobody had time to. Soon after, everything quieted down and the family just disappeared. Every last one of them. Poof! Gone. All their furniture, all their belongings, everything they owned, was left there untouched. People had been expecting quite a macabre scene when the rumors of the boy in the barn had reached Wicker. But there was no corpse tied up in the barn or hanging from its rafters. It was quite a disappointment after all that buildup, I can tell you. There were no bodies at all. It was as if they had vanished into thin air."

"Surely somebody saw them leave. There's only one way off the hill from what I've seen. And forgive me, but Wicker seems a very watchful place."

"Thin air. Poof!" His hand gestures were that of a magician. "There were rumors, of course. Some even said they had seen one of the children on the side of the hill, but nothing was ever substantiated."

"That all sounds like an urban legend to me, Mr. Craft," Chloe said.

"It's the story that's told." He shrugged his hangers. "Take it or leave it. But the family was strange. There's no denying that. Why, after the problems with the boy, the mother came into town—to this very library—and borrowed one of our oldest books. A book of the occult, witchcraft, spells, and the like. She never returned it. We don't loan out our older books anymore after that. One only has to learn that lesson once."

Chloe remembered the large leather book in Lana Pruitt's personal library. If Mr. Craft's story was true, it had to be the same volume of spells. It wasn't like there were many of them around, after all.

"And what about the big house?" she asked.

"For years, it was a summer home for a very wealthy man. In time, he got too old to care for the place, and it remained empty for some time, inviting only teenagers and vandals. Then the actress, Lana Pruitt—her, her husband, and her little girl—finally bought the old place and moved in."

Chloe's gaze was traveling. Remembering. "The girl died. I found her grave in the garden. Stumbled upon it by accident, really." She held up her hand before the librarian could speak. "I don't want to know how."

Mr. Craft seemed deflated, as if she had taken away his fun.

"No one ever knew what happened to the actress's husband, Michael. Like the family in the cottage, he was just gone one day. But there are rumors." He gave a sly look.

"That she killed him?"

"That she killed them both. Her husband and her daughter. That she was as crazy as the little boy decades earlier."

THE REMOTE control lay on his knee. The need to scratch was gone now. As Jeff sat slouched on the couch, trying to find something on the television, he didn't feel a thing aside from the diggings his own fingers had carved into his forearm, neck, and chest. Maybe there was something in the air here. Maybe he was allergic to some plant. It would have been odd, yes, being that he had been all over the world in his career and had never once had an allergic reaction to anything. Yet he was working in the dampness of a well. He had never done that before. Caves, yes. Wells, no.

Maybe that "something in the air" had gotten under his skin. That's exactly what it felt like: a crawling beneath his skin. And it was spreading. The air was packed with maybes.

Chloe was still in town. He was beginning to feel bad that he wished her away so often. But it was what it was. False happiness comes off as condescension. From an early age, Jeff was never able to pull any kind of performance out of that particular hat. His eyes always betrayed him. His best performances had always been in the sports arena.

He had come in from the well, if hesitantly, to take a small rest from his work. He was nearly at the bottom from what he could tell. He had used a flashlight and could see strewn treasures. Rusting relics. What project would he have to keep him busy after the well, though? That was a thought that made his heart beat a little faster like a sour excitement.

The TV was going in and out. Reception in the cottage wasn't the best. The power to the whole place had failed more than once. It had moved past annoying and on to expected by now. It seemed to annoy Chloe more than him.

Through the haze and fuzz of the television screen, Jeff was able to make out an older film. He knew immediately what it was. He'd seen it before, years ago. It was one of her most famous roles, the actress on the hill. The Unseen, one of those old Gothic thrillers filled with large houses, sparse lighting, and folded people. She looked younger, but it was still the actress. Her eyes were alive, though. Even through the struggling reception, Jeff saw the eyes. They were determined. She had lost those eyes now. She was merely existing these days. Her old eyes—the ones she wore in the film—had fallen to the floor and shattered.

He wondered if, higher up on the hill, the actress had power at all. If the cottage had issues with power, surely the big house did as well. Did she live by candlelight? Did she even have a television so she could watch her old films? By the looks of her on-screen, she was one of those types who enjoyed watching herself, or at least had been. But then, who didn't enjoy reliving past victories? He watched his own recorded ball games all the time.

The television hissed at him, flashing an impressionistic conglomeration of gray, black, and white. No. Not hissed. Laughed. Giggled. Giggled like a child in church.

The giggling. "Yeah, I heard it," he had wanted to tell Chloe in the barn. But he couldn't make himself admit that to her. He had his own theories about its source, and he was reticent to share them. That would mean a link, a new connection to his wife. That did not need to happen.

No. Chloe did not deserve to hear the giggling of the son she had killed. The son she had denied a father. So why, then, did she hear it?

The actress's face reappeared on the screen. She stared straight into Jeff. He didn't even try to hear what she was saying through the thick fog of sound. Her eyes glowed white. The power surged and then went out completely.

"Just as well," he said, still slouched. Still vacant. He scratched at his thigh.

Sitting there, the idea came to him that he should call his brother Ethan. They hadn't talked in so long. Not that they had ever really been close. But he was family and Jeff still cared about him. In fact, the reason he had never told Ethan about his diagnosis was because he didn't want his younger brother to worry.

The Jeep pulled up to the house.

Chloe, my wife, is home. My wife, Chloe, is home.

He felt that twinge of guilt again, the feeling that he was treating her too harshly. He knew any shrink would tell him it would be best to try and forgive. Reconnect with his brother and forgive his wife.

And then he remembered the giggles. A son. And he rose from the couch and walked out the back door to the well.

ETHAN WALKED the long corridor to his mother's room with a fresh bouquet of morning glories. These were his mother's favorite flower when she was cognizant. He brought a new bunch for her every week, purchased from the florist one block over. The late afternoon sky was dimmed, the last rays of sunlight streaming through the care facility's tall windows. It was a relatively quiet place. Only a few other visitors and the nurses walked the floors.

Ethan gave his obligatory nod and smile to one of his mother's caretakers in the hallway. "So nice to see you, Mr. Cane!" she said. "Every mother should be as lucky as to have a son like you."

Lucky? One son who couldn't even take care of his own mother and another who never saw her. That passed as luck?

He shut the door behind him and freshened up the vase. Old flowers out. New flowers in. "Hello, Mother," he said. He bent down and kissed her forehead.

She looked good. Restful, at least. Her silver hair was kept short and manageable, and she always wore her favorite nightgown. There was a closet full of them. She was well looked after here.

For a time after she was first put in the care facility, Ethan was always shocked when he came to visit her. She looked as if she might wake up at any moment. He had even sat in the very same chair he sat in now beside the bed and whispered through tears and clenched teeth, "Wake up, Mom! Wake up!"

He took the hairbrush from the dresser top and began lightly pulling it through her hair. He hoped it offered some type of comfort to her, somewhere deep inside.

"I'm sorry my husband and son couldn't come. You remember Kel and Bug? Life gets in the way. I promise, next time."

Ethan had been promising next times for years now. The truth was, he didn't want his child to see his grandmother like this. To have his only memory of her be that of a broken woman in a sterile room at a care facility? That was not the woman Ethan had grown up with. His mother could fight wild lions and then draw up a peace accord with them. She was a war settler. That was a quality Ethan lacked. Ethan held grudges and rarely acted to fix the matter that caused those grudges. Whenever he and Jeff argued as kids, his mother would sit them down until they had hashed things out. He hated those times. He couldn't help but feel she was always secretly siding with Jeff. He realized now that he should have learned from those occasions.

"Has Jeff been to see you lately, Mom?" It was a question with an answer that never changed. "I guess he lives too far away to get here very often, huh? I've been thinking about him a lot lately. I don't know why."

He took the brush and absentmindedly scratched at his forearm before returning it to his mother's silver hair.

"We weren't close as kids, but I do remember a couple times it almost seemed we were. I remember how, occasionally, for whatever reason, Jeff used to make me feel better after I had a rough day at school after the kids had teased me." Ethan smiled warmly with a bittersweet nostalgia. "We'd lay on the couch, his arm around me, and he'd say, 'Ethan, I don't care what anyone says about you. I think you're pretty cool.'" He laughed. "The jackass. And then, when Dad would go into one of his fits and blame me for everything, Jeff was right there. He wouldn't say anything. He'd just be there. And you. You, of course, were there too. I wish one of you would have said something. It makes me sad that…. But then, you never fought my battles, did you? You had your own war with Dad."

He grew more stoic. "And then, after the accident, Jeff left me to the state. I resented him so much for that. But in the end, it was for the best. I would never have met Kel if he hadn't…. I think I've been a bad brother, Mom. I think me and Jeff, we've been bad brothers to each other lately."

Hash it out, he heard her say. Sit your asses down and get it figured out. If you don't, who knows what that resentment will turn into. No dinner until you get this worked out. Understand?

He put the brush down and continued touching her hair with his hand. "I had one hell of a dream last week. I think that's what started this whole thing. It's why Jeff has been on my mind so much." He shuddered thinking about the nightmare.

"We were here, in the care facility. Except we were in the hall, and it was dark. There was nobody but you and me at first. You were wearing your hair like you did when we were kids, pulled back in a ponytail. I miss your long hair."

He took up the brush again.

"I was so happy to see you. But you… you looked sad. Worried. Even scared. The fluorescent lights flickered overhead all the way down the corridor. You know, like in those old movies when you know something bad is about to happen. Jeff always loved those movies. They scared the crap out of me. Still do.

"Anyway, at the other end of the corridor, just past this door, in fact, Jeff and Dad sat facing each other at a table. I don't think they saw either of us. But you were shouting. You were shouting at Jeff. I couldn't make out what you were saying, but you were terrified."

Ethan swallowed and leaned farther over his mother, as if imparting a secret but forgetting to whisper.

"And behind them… behind them, Mom, was this boy. I've never seen him before. Don't you have to have seen a person in real life for them to appear that clearly in a dream? I'm sure this guy was a complete figment, though, because I would have remembered that face. Even the rim of his farm hat couldn't hide the face—gaunt, pale, and eyes that seemed grown too large for his eye sockets. And he had a grin that…." Ethan shook and sat back in his chair.

"And then it went dark, and something tugged at my arm. I screamed and then I woke up. Bug was crying so I got up and sat with him for a while until he fell back to sleep. That was a good moment. Me and Bug, sitting up in the early hours. I don't know who was comforting who the most."

His mother was as serene as ever. Not that he expected her to wake up, but he hoped against hope for some sort of comfort. Some answer. It was then that he realized she had, in fact, given him one. Mother always knew what to do.

"I need to get hold of Jeff, don't I?"

SHE'S RIGHT THERE

CHLOE HAD felt underdressed when she arrived at the big house for tea. Lana answered the door in a long black velvet coat that fit perfectly around her still small waist. There was an ivory brooch of pink roses on a black beaded choker, and her blonde-and-silver hair was coifed for a night out, kinked and curled. She smelled of expensive perfume.

Chloe, on the other hand, wore an oversized gray sweatshirt with a bleach stain on the shoulder and rolled-up sleeves. She had on comfortable jeans and an old pair of sneakers. Her hair was tied back in a ponytail to keep it from whipping at her face. She blushed at her carelessness, but Lana didn't seem to notice.

Chloe was happy with her choice of apparel, however, once Lana had led her up the old stairs to the widow's walk. A small and unheated glass-enclosed cupola prepared Chloe to step once more into the wind. As they stepped out, the wind still bit, but the thick sweatshirt helped defend her.

Lana's face took a daily beating from the wind. Chloe could see it clearly now. Her face was dry and bruised pink. Chloe couldn't fathom staying up on the widow's walk for more than five minutes, much less coming up there every day. She became bleary-eyed from the wind to the point she had to wipe them before she looked through the telescope. Chloe drew a quick breath when she saw the strength of the telescope. If Lana were so inclined, she could spy quite a bit of what was happening at the cottage, and across the bay, homes could be seen in detail. Chloe felt intrusive and voyeuristic, yet she could not turn away.

"Not what you were expecting?" the actress said.

"Expecting?" Her voice shivered.

"I imagine you think me a crazy old woman who reads mysteries and has tea every day with crumpets while roasting in front of a fireplace. I do like tea, but I hardly ever sit down to drink it."

"I had no expectations."

Lana looked at her quite seriously. "That's dangerous," she said. "You should always expect something, my dear. How else will you protect yourself? Why, I could have brought you up here to throw you off and kill you. If you didn't expect it, you might deserve it."

Chloe backed away from the telescope. Whispers of rumors out-voiced the howling wind.

"Don't worry," Lana assured her. "I'm no killer." She said it with more warmth than Chloe had been accustomed to recently, and it calmed her. Still, she remained back against the house by the cupola door.

"It certainly is chilly here," Chloe said. "Not at all what I'm used to. I prefer humidity to frozen landscapes."

"Then what in the world are you doing here, my girl? It never gets warm here. Not even in summer. It's perpetually cold. You should have done your research." Lana trained her eyes out to sea. "There's nothing heavier than stone-cold sea."

The waves hit the rocks, another onslaught in their eternal role as combatants. The sound was lulling and peaceful, but there was, in fact, nothing peaceful about it. Beneath even the calmest of waters there was extreme violence, and in her travels, Chloe knew that well. The gulls above encouraged the war.

"How do you like the cottage?" Lana asked.

"It's... fine."

Lana gave a smirk. "You're too pretty to be a good liar. Pretty girls don't have to lie, so they don't get practice at perfecting the art. When pretty girls become liars, they give it a more respectable name. Like acting."

"It's not what I was hoping, all around. There's a strange mood about the place…. I have nightmares."

"Nightmares. Yes. I've never set foot on the property myself, but it still invades my dreams, like a little demon at the end of my path. A troll under the bridge that asks too much. My husband fixed that little cottage up again after years of neglect, you know."

"For your daughter."

"Yes. I told him to just let the thing crumble to dust, but she really wanted it and he wanted to do it for her. He was desperate for the cottage to be put to use again. He didn't want to rent it out to anyone either. He wanted it for Rebecca. It was their project. I wasn't here often enough for my protests to mean much anyway." She took a deep breath and stood up straight, deflecting memories. "He covered the well so she wouldn't fall into it and fixed up the place. She played house there. He would sometimes sleep down there with her, even when I was back from a film shoot. Jealousy is a twisting thing when its cause is a family member."

Chloe listened intently, only annoyed occasionally by the roar or touch of the wind. She was surprised Lana was opening herself so freely. Perhaps it was what the actress needed to do. Perhaps she had been waiting years for someone like Chloe to come along.

"Our daughter even had a friend. An imaginary one…." There was a note of question in her voice. "She called him the rascal. She said the cottage was his home first, but he would let her live there if she allowed him to do certain things…."

"What things?"

"I never found out. She died soon after." Lana's face became ugly for the first time since Chloe had met her. It dropped into a hideous frown, as if her whole face might melt away right there. But she stiffened her back once more and the ugliness left her. She was again the faded film star.

Suspicion was immediately cast on the husband in Chloe's mind and the things fathers should never do with their daughters.

"I've had nightmares ever since." Lana laughed with imposing self-judgment. "I had nightmares even before it all happened. I knew something was wrong. But I didn't act...." She turned to face Chloe. "Sometimes you have to sacrifice a great deal to save something much smaller but of much greater worth. I never made that sacrifice."

Chloe stared at her. It was as if the words the actress had said were in the air, staring Chloe down, saying Pay attention now.

"Let's head inside," Lana said. "You look like you're freezing to death."

JEFF LAY in the fetal position on the couch. He was in a pair of blue sweatpants and a plain white T-shirt. Lounging clothes. Lazy clothes. Sick clothes. The soles of his socked feet were still white. He hadn't felt well all day, like he was coming down with something. He felt he was on a ledge and about to fall over. Whichever way he fell would be bad. He wondered if this is how his father felt before he killed himself. Was this the disease? Would he only feel worse from here on out?

The TV fuzzed and jabbered in front of him. Again, he wasn't really paying attention to it. What he did hear—a news program—warned of a snowstorm coming from the east. Snowstorms didn't bother him. He had once led an adventure tour of thirteen through a range of treacherous snow-covered mountains without a single injury or accident occurring.

Jeff couldn't remember the last time he was sick. It had to have been before his parents had their accident. He couldn't afford to be sick after that. He had to take care of things, not only immediately after in terms of funeral and interment arrangements for his dad, but also working with the state in finding his mother proper care and taking care of Ethan in the longer term. The state was a draining and often heartless entity. But Jeff knew how to fight. Three years on the wrestling team had honed him. He made sure where Ethan lived and where their mother was cared for were within a few miles of each other.

He was eighteen when the accident happened, and somehow, quite improbably, had gained guardianship of Ethan, who was sixteen at the time. It helped that their parents were financially safe and intelligent. There was a nice savings, enough to help Ethan, when the time came, to head to college. The rest they could get through government grants. Jeff decided Ethan had to go to college.

Jeff, however, was not the college type. He hadn't the time for it. When he'd left to go adventuring, he had no intention of being gone for two years. Then he met Chloe with the adventure tour outfit. Things started to seem different. Hopeful. He was no longer flailing. Chloe convinced her mother to give him a job, and there were joint adventure trips to Spain, to Australia, to islands they had never heard of. But Chloe would never go anywhere too cold with him. She hated the cold seasons of the world, the frigid mountains and desolate, icy plains of the north.

Jeff turned over on his back but kept his head turned toward the television. He watched the picture fade in and out and listened for more warnings. He began to drift, his eyes closing and opening in fades and starts.

The dreams had been strange lately. So strange. Chloe had mentioned them as well when she was still attempting some sort of reconciliation.

Staring into the snowy reception, Jeff could just make out a face formed by the blizzard of dots and lines. He squinted harder and saw a young boy with large eyes. And the boy was smiling.

He giggled, and Jeff fell asleep.

WHEN CHLOE arrived back at the cottage, it was dark. She had, up until this point, avoided being outside at night, but having stayed too long at the big house, it was unavoidable that she would need to travel downhill in the dark cold. The cliff and sea were open and overwhelming to one side of her, the trees closed in and watching on the other. At least Chloe could feel something watching her, numerous shadow people under the trees. She thought of the fiddler but then pushed him back in her mind. She kept her eyes to the ground and hurried, arms folded, to the cottage. She calmed her nerves by recounting the films of Lana's she had seen. Four that she could recall, and she was surprised it had even been that high. She did her best to remember their plots, their cast, anything. The walk home was in many ways a long prayer. A meditation.

When at last inside the cottage, she breathed, but it was not a sigh of relief, just the realization that the monsters inside were a change from the monsters out.

Jeff was asleep on the couch. He slept out by the TV more and more often lately. This was good and bad.

Good: The discomfort between them wasn't carried into their bedroom as they lay beside one another and tried to get to sleep.

Bad: She was alone in that bed… in that room… in this cottage.

The remote lay on the floor, Jeff's hand dangling over it, the buttons just out of reach. The television light flashed, and mumbles of a weather forecast could be heard but vaguely. Chloe went around the room, turning off lights. She left the television on but set it to mute. She waited a minute before she turned for the bedroom. She needed to collect her courage first. The bedroom always seemed darker than the rest of the cottage. It enveloped and possessed.

"Why are you still here?" she chided herself.

A creak somewhere in the cottage made her quickly dash for the room and flick on the light. Thank God for electricity.

As she got herself dressed for bed, she thought of Lana. Of how they spent hours in the old library—or rather, the gathering of books in what Lana called the library—looking over old manuscripts. Chloe had never seen books as old as some of those Lana possessed. They had traveled through thousands of hands and most likely passed before millions of eyes, good, bad, and indifferent. The books Lana seemed to pause on the longest—those that gave Chloe the unholiest of chills—were the books on the occult. That included the large leather book that seemed to be the centerpiece of the entire collection.

"We'll look through this someday, you and me," Lana had said. "It was a gift to me from Rebecca. I think you would find it quite interesting. Useful, even."

Chloe thought that was a strange statement for the actress to make. But then, Lana was not an average person. She was, at heart, an actress and made many such cryptic statements, whether she believed in them or not. They were lines. They all hung in the air, having nowhere else to go.

In bed, the lights off, Chloe steeled herself against her surroundings. The darkness here was still frightening, but she was beginning to get used to it, if not comfortable with it. Everything—every noise, whether creak or bump—was blamed on the winds up from the sea. Scratches were but the trees. Moans were Jeff asleep on the couch. She knew better, but at the moment, she could not do better. She would leave in the spring. That was the best she could do.

And the eyes? What of the watching she felt from the windows and the corners of the room? The shadow people. How did she explain that? She chose not to. She didn't think about the watching. She found that if she emptied her mind, she could even get to sleep. She just needed to open herself up to the possibility of sleep. Let it come into her like she was a vessel.

It was a voice—not a fiddle—that made her rise this time. She was on the very edge of sleep, at that forgotten moment when one at last slips under sleep's veil. That moment one cannot exactly remember when they awake the next morning. A high-pitched voice came from the front room.

"Will you do me a favor?"

More than mischief, it sounded malevolent. Like angled brows and wrenching hands.

Chloe sat up immediately, her confusion at its peak. Her heart pumped feverishly the ice-cold blood through her veins. She sat in the dark, wondering if perhaps she had imagined it all. If it were the remnants of a nightmare. Please be a nightmare!

But then she heard the giggle.

She leapt to her feet and crept to the bedroom door. She peered out, but saw nothing. Her breath was quick and deep, and her heart shook her body with its beats. She was an anxious orchestra. The darkness swallowed the front room. She would have to inch out of the bedroom to see anything with even minor clarity. The electricity had gone out again sometime during the night, so the television was now off. She kept to the wall, slowly making her way closer to the front of the cottage. She realized too late that she had nothing to defend herself with if there was someone else in the house.

As she approached the couch, every footfall an echoing alarm, the natural light from outside let her see her husband's chest rising and falling. She looked around the room, swallowing back her fear, and noticed nothing unusual.

At once, the television picture came back on, its white blur defining the room.

Then from Jeff's own lips, she heard the voice that had woken her: "She's right there."

It was the same menacing tone she had heard before, and she took a step back from it. She thought about waking Jeff up, literally shaking him as bad as he had shaken her. But she let him lie in his enigmatic dreams. She wasn't certain she wanted to know what it was he was dreaming about. Still, she stood over him a moment longer, the hairs on her body rising and prickling. He said nothing more.

Chloe knew she wouldn't get any sleep tonight. At least not until there was a bit of light in the sky. The power was on, so she went to the kitchen, turned on the light, and got online. There had to be someone she could chat with on one of the messenger services. Someone back home. She put on the headphones and mic. They buffered the nighttime creaks and groans of the kitchen.

"Someone. Anyone," she pleaded.

The glow from the computer screen washed over her. She felt encased, almost as if it were a defense from the dark. From everything that wasn't in the false light. Names appeared on her chat list. Most of their icons and avatars were gray and sleeping. Only a few of her acquaintances were on or even cared to talk. Ethan was there. His little yellow icon grinned at her next to his handle: Ethanlives4Bug.

She didn't move. She waited, uncertain as to what to do. His response, even if it were negative, would be better than the silence that threatened to burst her eardrums.

As she sat there waiting to contact him, a box popped up on the screen telling her that Ethan wanted to chat with her via the webcam and asking if she would accept. It's now or never, she thought and clicked Yes.

Instantly Ethan's face appeared in a small window on the laptop's screen. He looked much the same as he had the last time she had seen him two years ago. The same angular features and his hair was the same responsible length of black. He wore a white button-up shirt that gleamed in the computer light. Ethan was chatting in the dark. He looked at her pensively.

There was an awkward pause. A moment of recognition, of half smiles and forced pleasantries beneath which lay fields of questions.

"I've made friends with the actress who lives on top of the hill. Lana Pruitt."

"Lana Pruitt is your neighbor?" His eyes widened and his voice pitched.

Chloe grinned. "She is. She used to own the cottage as well."

"What's she like?" Chloe saw Ethan relax a little. His shoulders eased.

"Distant... and sad." And familiar. "She's had quite the horror story of her own since she quit acting in them. When Jeff and I first met her, I thought she was a little batty. Now I think she's just lonely."

Ethan tensed up once again. "Is that Jeff?" he asked, peering past Chloe.

Chloe had heard no sign of Jeff rising from the couch. No extra creaks from the aching floor. She looked behind her and saw nothing. Just the empty kitchen doorway and the darkness of the front room.

"I don't think he's up."

When she looked back around, Ethan seemed stricken. "No," he said. "No. It wasn't him at all."

"What's wrong?" She knew true concern when she saw it. It was akin to terror. Like a radiating blight that started in your core and spread outward.

"Nothing. I just thought I saw... nothing." That look. That accusatory look.

"Ethan, there are things.... I see things—"

"Listen, I'll try and get up there to see you soon, Chloe. Okay? I'll try to get up there very soon. I think something—"

But he was cut off midsentence. The power hiccupped and the image on the computer screen blipped into black. Chloe sat in the darkness as silent and still as she could. She listened to her own breathing and the winds outside. She closed her eyes tightly. There it was, the fiddle, making the hairs on her neck bristle as if someone were blowing directly on them.

Slowly, she turned in her seat and looked into the front room. There was nothing. The faint light from the window was now all that could be seen. Yet there was movement in the shadows. She heard it but could not see it clearly. She frantically searched in front of her. Her breaths quickened.

Then, at last, she saw it. A form. A shoulder betraying position, silhouetted near the window. She wanted to scream, but all she could etch out was a broken "Jeff." She tried to calm herself. She listened harder for a frozen moment.

The floor creaked. It snapped.

Chloe jumped from her seat, intending to dash for the bedroom. Her nightgown caught on the chair and pulled it to the floor, knocking her on the back of the knee as it fell. She collapsed with a scream.

When the commotion had ended, her hand was resting on a foot. The recognition of the feel of flesh sent her into a panic. She recoiled immediately and crawled back into a corner shouting her husband's name in desperate pleas.

"It's me!" he said through the barrage of cries. "It's me. Chloe! What the hell's wrong with you?"

She could just make out his face as her eyes adjusted. It was cast in strips of twilight blue.

"I hate it here, Jeff," she said. "I hate this goddamn place we're in."

WHEN CHLOE disappeared from the computer screen, Ethan sat bewildered. She wouldn't have just quit the chat, would she? The feelings between them were never warm, but neither did they warrant being rude.

He checked her status. All of her icons and avatars were gray or sleeping. She was offline. That much was certain. Most likely she had been thrown off. From what he gathered in the mass e-mail he was sent before they had moved, Jeff and Chloe now lived up in the hills. Maybe things didn't work as well up where there. Atmospheric conditions. Clouds and the like. Technology was amazing, but it couldn't fix everything. There were some barriers it couldn't break through. Not just yet.

Still, Ethan sat anxious and alert. His fingers danced over the keys on his computer. He was using the desktop in the living room. He never used his laptop for chatting. The laptop was strictly for school. He waited to see if Chloe's icon might pop back up. Ethan needed a bit of reassurance. The last thing he had seen before the screen went black had frightened him, set the worry tight in him, like a stone tied around his gut.

If he had seen right, if it wasn't a mirage from a mischievous webcam connection, there had been someone standing right behind Chloe. A figure in shadow. There was movement to it anyway. He'd assumed it was Jeff at first, but then….

But then….

Much too thin. Much too thin to be Jeff. Jeff had the athletic body of a man who did what he did: adventure sports. The rakish form standing behind Chloe was anything but fit. This led Ethan to one of two conclusions, both of which turned his stomach while inducing supreme rage:

Chloe was cheating on Jeff again, or

Jeff was much more ill than Ethan had suspected and that was indeed him behind Chloe, wasting away. This meant Chloe was lying to him for some reason.

Both of these options made Ethan want to pick up the phone and demand to know what was going on. He headed to the kitchen and downed a hefty gulp of Pepto-Bismol.

The more he thought about the form in the dark, the more the imagined face flipped from Jeff, then to some phantom lover, then to… to what? There was something familiar about that shadow, that particular figure. He had seen it before at the end of a dream hallway.

Ethan shivered. Yes. He would definitely make it up there to see Jeff very soon. He'd try to call before that. He did not like the thought of Chloe there alone with Jeff if indeed he was ill. Tomorrow he'd put in a request for a short leave at the high school where he taught history. They would be able to find a good substitute. The academic year had just started, but surely they would understand. After all, this was a matter of family.

FROM HER window in the room she used for a library on the first floor of the house, Lana could not see through the trees to the cottage. If she were the type, she could simply climb the stairs to the telescope to perceive if they too were experiencing a power failure once again. She knew they were, of course, so that a trip up to the widow's walk would only mean one thing: that she had concerns for another human being, namely Chloe.

Lana had candles at the ready for those occasions when the power went out. She never put them in storage. They were as much residents of the house as she, congregating in the halls and on the mantelpieces. The library was scattered with them, all of them tall, slender, and the same eggshell white. There were three near the sofa, one on the eastern windowsill, one by the door, and one—the largest one—at the center of the table where the large book of spells lay opened.

She had thought many times about "calling forth." The tools for it were already laid out and had been for weeks. She had done a séance once before, alone, with only herself, the candles, and the big book. There had been a few rattling windows and flickering flames, but nothing else to indicate a presence. She believed it would work now, however. She believed in a couple of new things now. This time, she sat down with determination. The book was spread before her like a wide plain, the words like hills to climb over, line by line. The flames cast their shadows, and the actress squinted as she spoke:

"I call forth the spirit of… Rebecca Kinsar. My daughter Rebecca. Speak to me."

Silence but for the wind outside.

Again, she called forth. Again, nothing. Lana furrowed her brow. She had so wanted this to work. The waiting, the listening was harder than anything she had ever done. As an actress, she had patience. Hours on film sets would give you that. But she was tired of waiting. Waiting for Michael to come back. Waiting for resolution. Hearing nothing but the wind and the *tick tick tick* of the stout clock on the mantel.

She slammed her open hand on the table as a mother would when exasperated with a child. "Come to me, Rebecca!"

At last, there was the smallest of somethings. Not a noise, but a dangerous quiet. A quiet that might have existed before the world came into being. The hiss before the bang. Lana wondered if she had done something terribly wrong. She looked from one corner of the library to the other. The candle at the center of the table fizzled out as if pressed between two fingers. Lana watched its last embers fade before she noticed a form through the smoke directly opposite her.

She jumped from her chair, screaming. This was what she had wanted, but not how she had wanted it. There was her little girl, Rebecca, but not in the form she had known her in life. Instead, the child was the twisted, broken mess Michael had told her of one night, the heap of spoiled sweetness he had described in drunken disgust and regret.

"Where's my little girl?" Lana shouted. She clutched at the back of the chair she now stood behind. "Why are you like this?"

The girl's head, broken on its neck and lying to the side, let out a gurgling mess of sounds. Lana screamed once more, tears dripping down her face.

Rebecca breathed out, "He doesn't want you there."

"What?"

"You can't ever go there, or he'll come here. You can't ever go there, Momma. Never."

Lana quickly reached forward and slammed the book closed. "Leave!" she said. "I'm sorry, but please leave."

The child receded into the dark as if she had never been there at all, and the deadly quiet left the room to a more acceptable silence. Lana collapsed to the floor and sobbed, rocking with intermittent screams.

THE WOMAN & THE HILL

THE BACK door slammed shut. Jeff had risen early, most likely to work on his well project. Chloe heard him shuffling around in the front room as she lay in bed. It wasn't until he went outside that she finally felt some relief. It was as if she had been holding her breath all night. Waiting. She felt the pressure in her chest dissipate in a rush.

She had been awake for a while now, long enough to see the daylight slink into the room. The dreams were not letting her be. They were of people she had never known. When she was able to see them clearly through the impressionistic folds of the dream, their faces were tired and scared. Last night she had dreamed of two young boys and a woman, apparently their mother. Yet she knew it was not a dream, but rather a memory. Old homes store them in their walls and floorboards.

There were so many things for Chloe to feel awkward about. She listed them in her head: the events of the night before, including the conversation with Ethan; the startling voice that both was and wasn't Jeff; and her midnight admission to her husband that she wasn't happy. She might have lain in her bed and stewed over these things all day if her cell phone hadn't chimed.

The reception on Bad Luck Hill, like the power, was untrustworthy, but this morning it was at least fathomable. It was the chatty librarian, Mr. Craft. The archivist had been in, he told her, and had found what she had wanted. It was on a table, waiting for her.

"No trouble at all," he said before she spoke a word.

She got dressed and left without telling Jeff where she was headed. There was really only one place she could go. To town. Where else but to town?

The cold season was headed in. The air was crisp and demanding. The temperature had dropped in the night and refused to climb again. A storm was coming and the cold was its regalia. Chloe wrapped up tight and looked across the waters as she drove into Wicker. The desolate seascape in the morning was the graveyard of ships and echoes. Shout forever and you'll never be heard.

Books and old newspapers were spread out, as promised, on a solid oak table when she arrived at the library. There wasn't much in the way of archival material on Bad Luck Hill, but Mr. Craft looked pleased with himself anyway. He stood at the door waiting, his hands pressed in a steeple.

"If there's anything else you need," he said, leaning in too closely as she sat down, "just let me know." He left her on her own, though she could feel his eyes watching her constantly. He had laid the materials on a table close to the front desk, so she was always in his sight.

What information there was came in the form of birth certificates, land deeds, and death announcements. Nothing very odd or suspicious. The hill was initially under the ownership of the town's namesake, a man named Alvus Wicker. He had kept it for quite a long time and had died at the age of one hundred and two. It had passed on through a few generations before slipping out of the Wicker hands completely in the early twentieth century, by which point, the big house was already close to two hundred years old and the cottage had been built as a home for the groundskeeper and his family.

The big house was then sold to a wealthy Indiana family named Clemson, who used it for a summer getaway, and the cottage was rented to various people for various reasons. None of them stayed longer than a few years. Some were gone within a couple of months. The turnover was exceedingly high. In the 1950s, a family named Raskin moved into the cottage and stayed for some time longer than any of the previous inhabitants. They were a mother, father, two sons, and one daughter. The daughter, Sybil, was the youngest and the only family member named in the archives. The father had died, according to a newspaper clipping where he was referred to as "Mr. Hill," of a flu.

Two sons. Chloe looked up from the ledger of names and dates. Mr. Craft was busy elsewhere in the library. She remembered the dream she had had from the night before. Two boys fighting. One, the healthier-looking of the two, seemed to have a significant advantage, but the other, the skinnier and sickly looking one, was winning out of pure viciousness. The skinny one had beaten the other until the healthier boy was nearly unconscious and was being dragged down to No Hope Creek. The skinny boy was laughing. Giggling. The boy being dragged moaned and whimpered.

Then they were in the creek and the hurt boy was being held under. He was alert now and thrashing, but the other held him hard. Then a wiry-haired woman—their mother, it seemed—raced down the hill to the creek. She pulled the sickly boy off the other, screaming and shrieking.

Chloe shivered and brought in her shoulders, as if there were wings attached to them that might shield her from cold or harm.

At last, she came to it. The death of the crazy boy. She didn't know which one of the boys it had been, and it seemed, neither did the town. He was just a child, after all, and children were never as interesting as adults. His death was listed as a suicide, yet from what Mr. Craft had told her, no one had even seen the boy or his body after he was tied up in the barn. No one knew for certain he was dead. But it made a good story.

Jeff had spent a lot of time in that barn. He was most likely in that barn or working on the well this moment. Jeff and Death.

After the boy's suicide, there was no more mention of the Raskin family. They just disappeared. Not one word of their whereabouts. The big house emptied soon after and wasn't inhabited again until Lana Pruitt bought it in the early 1980s. The cottage was then renovated for Rebecca's playhouse, but no one actually lived there again until she and Jeff purchased it. They were already listed in the archives. They were the present and the past.

The only other odd happening on Bad Luck Hill was the tragic death of Rebecca and the disappearance of her father. The latter might not even be included on that list of the strange. For all anyone knew, Michael had left Lana and was as guilty of the child's death as Chloe was beginning to suspect.

Chloe leaned back in her chair. Seven suspicious disappearances. An entire family of five and two of another. And everything within her vicinity.

She closed her eyes, remembering the dream. The skinny boy shook violently as his mother had rebuked him and she headed back to the cottage with his brother. He stood for a moment, staring at the stream in front of him. There would be a thrashing to come. He picked up the large-brimmed hat that had been knocked off during play, and then he turned and looked directly at the dreamer. He stared right at Chloe. And he grinned, eyes as big and bulging as two hard-boiled eggs. She had awoken with a catch of her breath.

Having discovered everything she could from the archives, Chloe approached the librarian, who was now back at the front desk. "I was noticing," she said, "that the little girl is the only Raskin named in any of the papers. Is there a reason for that?"

"Sure there is," Mr. Craft said, looking up at her with eyes urging gossip. "She was the only one any of the townsfolk knew by name. She was the only one who would answer when asked for it. At first. But that soon changed. It didn't take long before she was as hush as the rest of them. That's what I'm told. Yes. That's just what the others tell me."

Jeff tied the yellow rope around the strongest of the trees close to the barn. The barn itself, he decided, did not look as trustworthy as he first thought it was. He pulled on his thick working gloves to reduce rope burn and flipped on his cave helmet's light. Using the rope and his climbing gear—a pick and his crampons—he would slowly crawdaddy down the well.

With a hop, he entered the mouth of the well. It was just narrow enough for him to safely and comfortably stretch out an arm and touch the opposite side. The shift in the air was immediate, a clinging, cold dampness. Every sound and scrape he made was amplified by the cavern below him. He imagined when it rained, before the well was covered by the slab and the stone, it had held a good deal of water. Now only the stones that it was constructed of showed any signs of wetness. Pebbles and the loose detritus that fell as he descended down the sides of the well did not hit water. Rather, they hit something solid.

Nausea and vertigo hit him, and he had to close his eyes to still himself. The truth was, he felt like a dog. As mangy and sick as one anyway. He scratched like he had fleas. His body was red with the marks. The unpleasantness was like that of a tarantula bite, only turned up. And he felt like something more was gnawing at him, like it had gotten inside and was now making a wreck of his guts and his head.

And then there was Chloe's crack about not liking—no, the word was hating—where they were at. What did that mean? She was the one who had chosen the place, after all. But then, he was the one falling in love with it. It figured she would want to leave.

He lowered himself farther. Faint glints shone from well debris at the bottom. He was still too far up to see what lay in the gut of the well. Into the dark. Into the dark.

He was so ill. So fucking sick, tired, and ready to retch. He knew he had slept plenty the night before, but he couldn't remember the last time he had woken up well-rested. He threw up acidic spittle, and it left a metallic taste in his mouth. He heard it smack the debris below.

Earth dwellers. Spiders and worms wriggled and crawled past him. Occasionally a spider would dart across his hand as he placed it on the wall for support. A scant and fleeting notion of paranoia swept over him, of spiders everywhere, watching him. Waiting for him to slip and become their meal.

He looked up. The light was slipping away, becoming a tiny sphere overhead. What if he fell? What if he didn't have the strength to pull himself back up? Could he even be heard all the way down there?

He was sweating profusely. It stung his eyes and tasted dirty on his lips. Suddenly, it didn't seem like such a good idea to be in the well. What if he fell? What if he screamed and screamed and Chloe never heard him? Or worse: what if she did but chose not to answer?

Death. Last night he'd had a dream about death. Ethan was trying to kill him by No Hope Creek. Ethan, the epitome of gentility, a fratricidal maniac.

Jeff was near the bottom now. His light caught a glint of something shiny. There wasn't as much refuse as he had thought there would be. No great treasure that he could see at any rate. That was a bit disappointing. The air was thicker down there, and there was a stench, the primeval smell of earth.

He reached for the object that welcomed the helmet light, the first beam of brightness it had most likely seen in some time. It looked to be a little pony, crystal or blown glass. As Jeff touched it, the light exposed something else as well—a hand, badly decomposed. Jeff jerked away, nearly losing his traction on the wall. He adjusted the beam's focus. Lying there at the bottom of the well, a crumpled and broken heap, was the body of a man. His face was a distorted nightmare, with a jaw that stretched as if in the midst of a scream. It watched in the direction of the glass pony, and also, it seemed, watched Jeff as well.

FROM THE telescope on the widow's walk, Lana had been watching Jeff stare down the well's mouth for days. Perhaps he was gathering the courage to go into the dark. Though a deficiency of courage seemed highly unlikely given his choice of career. It seemed more plausible that he was daring whatever lay in the well's depths not to match his own gilded imaginings.

When at last he did journey inward, burrowing into Bad Luck Hill, Lana watched with mounting anxiety. She did not know from where this sudden anxiousness came, but it rested around her as sure as the embrace of her own arms on her shoulders. Tighter and tighter. She held her breath to shallow rhythms until Jeff reappeared. He held nothing, but upon emerging, he sat on the edge of the well's mouth and peered into the cavern, his headgear still bright and shining down. He did not move for some time, as still as the broken cherub in the garden.

It was getting later in the day. Lana found herself moving slowly down the stairs to the porch. Her teeth chattered and she clenched her jaw to stop them. She hurriedly searched the library for the small pair of silver binoculars given to her as a gift from a former director, the image of Jeff sitting on the well mouth held frozen in her mind. When she reached the porch, however, he was gone again. She sat down on a rocker, her back straight, her body alert, and kept watch.

What was it? Why was she so interested in what he was doing? Something was different about today. Something was coming. Her teeth chattered on and her flesh crawled. It was in the air. It was all around her.

Jeff hadn't gone down the well again as Lana had thought. He came out of the house with what looked like a stiff sleeping bag. A stretcher. Again, something most likely familiar to him from his choice of career. The sight of it made Lana gasp aloud. She covered her mouth as if someone might hear her. What else would a stretcher be used for, she thought, but a body.

Lana was fascinated as she peered through the binoculars, making her way from the rocker to the edge of the porch, as Jeff fastened ropes to the strange white cot and lowered it down the well. He tied the rope to a different tree than the one he himself was secured to, and then slowly and carefully, he disappeared once more.

By this time, Lana was off the porch, treading through the uncut grass and onto the gravel road she had seen Chloe use so many times now. It was a good distance from the big house to the cottage for her, and steep. Somehow, the road felt colder and stranger than Lana had known it in her life. An ill wind rushed at her up the gradient. Soon she was as far away from her own home as she had been in twenty years. The sky was darkening and the waters were placid, a day ripe with frowns.

She stopped in the middle of the road in front of the cottage just as Jeff's helmet light began piercing up and out of the well. A solitary beam of light coming from the core of the hill as focused as true intent. If the very mouth of Hell had opened up, Lana was certain this was what it would look like.

Jeff climbed out of the well with a violent cough, unaware of Lana standing just a few feet away, and he began to haul the cot up after him. It seemed a difficult task as he grunted and growled. The rectangular cot was dragging against the sides of the circular well, but at last it rose from the dark. Jeff carefully placed the cot on the ground in front of the well and folded back the covering that had kept its contents in place.

The corpse's face, not completely gone of emotion, was enough to make Lana stumble. The shirt—a shocking blue button-up that Michael would never have bought for himself—rushed back to her in Christmas Day memories some thirty years past. And then she saw the little glass pony in his grasp....

Jeff had still not seen Lana. He crouched, studying the figure with his head lantern. The light added shades and definitions of horror. It was not until Chloe came out the back door that he finally noticed anything more about his surroundings.

"What did you find?" Chloe said. Then seeing Lana, she stopped short in surprise.

Jeff quickly stood and watched the actress as she struggled near the corpse of her husband, Michael. Jeff's helmet light cast its spotlight on her.

Chloe neared slowly as well. "What's wrong?"

And then she too saw the body and its condition, and she turned away with a shriek.

"He was in the well," Jeff said in a near whisper. He wiped his forehead of sweat.

Lana bent and touched her husband's tormented face gently. Then she took the pony from his grip. "You mean, you never left me?" she said, her voice a pitiful echo of a wind. "You were here the whole time?"

THE ACTRESS stood with her rifle at her side as her husband was interred beside Rebecca in the garden. Chloe thought that the maimed cherub that guarded the little girl's grave seemed balanced at last. Jeff and Chloe attended without being specifically asked. After all, someone needed to. A body so long lost with none of the respect due it, no fresh dirt to help send it back to the whole, needed some kind of special attention.

"We'll plant him by Rebecca," Lana had said with a voice of grief that was foreign to what Chloe had grown accustomed to hearing from the actress. Lana now spoke with a certain pride in her loss, a tangible amount of relief that Michael had not, as she had imagined for many years, left her. In seeing that, Chloe felt shame that she ever thought the woman could have had a hand in her husband's death. She had thought just what the town of Wicker had wanted her to think. They'd needed her to feed them. To feed their fascination with the woman and the hill.

There the three stood. The wind was the only thing that dared make a sound in the dead and browned garden. Jeff held the shovel. He was dressed modestly, jeans and a respectable Sunday shirt he had never worn before. Chloe was more formal, wearing a long black skirt, a white blouse, and a dark waistcoat like someone from a past age. She stood across the grave from Jeff with Lana in the middle, emotionless and burdened, her rifle like a walking stick at her side.

There was no marker. Not even a creek stone. Lana knew he would always be there. There was no real ceremony. Whatever god Lana had once prayed to had abandoned her, and she spit at him every night before she went to sleep. It was her one kept tradition.

She thanked Jeff for all the work he had done on Michael's behalf. It was he who had gone to town to find a coffin, and it was he who had done the digging. She had prepared a meal for them to show her gratitude.

"Not so far down," the actress whispered at her husband's coffin. "Stay nearer to the ground for me this time."

The rifle was for everyone else in the world. For those curious townsfolk who tried sneaking up the hill to feed their bloody imaginings. For the press who had gotten wind that the fallen movie star had found her husband's corpse in a well. And perhaps, most of all, for Michael's family, or what remained of it—a sister who had been an annoyance to Lana since the day the actress and Michael, a carpenter by trade, had married. This rifle was for his sister's lily white forehead if she so much as stepped into Lana's view on Bad Luck Hill.

Now that Lana had finally begun roaming the grounds, and with a firearm no less, she emerged as a formidable woman. In the days before the burial, Chloe had heard the rifle fire numerous times and had even witnessed Lana nearly hit her target once.

"Come back and I'll shoot your balls off!" she shouted at the terrified trespasser. She would have done it too. Lana, it seemed to Chloe, was now protecting rather fiercely her husband and daughter, both of them back in her company after being lost for so long. She would not abide any gossipmonger or family member trying to take a bit of what she had cried and mourned over for so many years.

The Wicker townsfolk, who climbed the hill in slow increments like zombies from the type of B-movie Lana had got her start in, were deterred but not totally stopped. Their rise up Bad Luck Hill had a viral determination.

"You won't really kill anyone, will you?" Chloe had asked once.

"The hell I won't. They're climbing for their own graves. I've got the law on my side. That's trespassing, plain and simple. They've got ill intent, and I'm just protecting what's mine. I don't want them so much as looking at my house with their beady little eyes that they mask behind their quaint shop windows."

This passion for guarding her dead was evidenced at the burial when a helicopter flew overhead. Lana looked up, at first in disbelief and then in anger. She took her rifle and left the garden, heading into the house with broad steps. Chloe looked at Jeff, who offered her no explanation. She followed the actress up the stairs to the widow's walk.

"Lana! You don't know if they were trying to get a look at the burial. Maybe it's just sightseers."

The helicopter was hanging too low, too near the big house, like a red apple to be plucked. Lana raised the rifle and fired. She

"Chloe?" he said, his voice strained through the distance and the wires.

"Hello, Ethan." She tried to sound pleased to see him. She was afraid her voice came off as nervous, though. "How is everything? Your husband? The baby?"

"They're fine. We're all fine."

The mention of the baby brought things to the fore, but they both ignored the subject. The fragile floor might give way if they jumped too hard.

"How's Jeff?" Ethan asked.

"He's asleep on the couch. He hasn't been feeling well today." She omitted the fact that he hadn't been sleeping in the bed for a while, as it was none of Ethan's business. "I don't think it's anything serious. Maybe a cold." She paused. "You look good, Ethan."

"Thanks. So do you." His brown eyes gazed at her with an intensity she always found unnerving.

"It's a real nice place. You should come for a visit." It was more of an uncertain question than anything. A space filler. She realized too late that by putting it out there, she was only inviting more discomfort into her life.

"You like it there?"

"Um… yeah. I mean, like every new place, it has its problems. I suppose I—we—just need to get used to its quirks and kinks."

"How is Jeff dealing with the time off from work?"

"He's keeping himself busy. There's an old well that comes with the place. He's cleaning it out. I can only imagine what he's going to find once he gets to the bottom. People throw all kinds of things in wells."

"And you? How are you keeping busy?"

She felt the jibe. Even though Jeff and Ethan hadn't talked for a while, Ethan had to have heard of her indiscretion.

had done it so fast that Chloe had no time to try and stop her, and fell backward in shock. Lana fired again and the chopper veered sideways, fleeing for safer sky.

"That ought to tell them just how serious I am," she said. She scanned the hill with the telescope. When she saw a suspicious lump in the bushes, she fired at it too. The lump grew legs and tumbled down the hill.

Lana turned to Chloe, who watched her, eyes wide and mouth agape. Chloe's hands had instinctively flown up to protect her ears from the sound of rifle fire and still hung frozen in the air.

"This," Lana said, looking at the platform on which they stood, "this will never happen again. I'll never use this wretched widow's walk ever again. Now, come." She walked past Chloe and into the house. "Let us have a proper wake."

JEFF HAD been feeling worse that day. The bug that he had caught—for he was certain that's what it was—was not going away. This was his fault for not taking better care of himself. Golden boys were hardly invincible anymore. He felt chills at the burial, and though the strangeness of the event was not lost on him, he did not watch the goings-on with any real interest. He found himself more concerned with Chloe, with their matters of the heart. Since he had brought up Michael's corpse, he had been thinking quite a bit about Chloe. About them.

It was evening and he stood at the kitchen door wrapped in a blanket and shivering. He had vomited earlier, and Chloe had commented on how pale he looked. The itching had spread as well, making him mark up his legs and his face.

"It comes and goes," he said. "Hour by hour, it goes from crap to shit and then back to crap."

He watched her make chicken noodle soup for him on the old stove. It was from a can, and she was never very good in the kitchen, but there was caring there. More than he had shown to her in the past year. She stirred it with a wooden spoon, gently, her wrist swirling a delicate dance, and then she brought the bowl to the table.

"Sit," she said.

Jeff pulled himself from the spot at the door with effort and plodded to the table. He sat down with an unsteady plop.

"There's more down there," he said.

"In the well?" she asked uneasily.

"Yeah. I still haven't reached the bottom. I'm close, but there might be buried treasure yet. Buried secrets."

"Or maybe it's just garbage. Maybe everything thrown down there is broken and missing pieces."

"Except Michael."

"Except him."

"Do you think we're like them?" Jeff asked, swirling the soup and playing with the noodles. "Like the actress and her husband?"

"How do you mean?" Chloe sat opposite him, excited by the first real opportunity for a conversation with him in ages.

"They seemed so disconnected. She thought he had left her, but all this time he was only a few yards away…. Is that us?" He looked up, his eyes straining to meet hers.

Chloe bit her lip, trying desperately to keep eye contact. "I don't know. Maybe?"

"I don't want that to be us."

"What are you saying, Jeff? Do you want to…?"

"Try again." He took a sip of the soup and grimaced. Still cold. "Maybe."

"What would I have to do to make you understand how sorry I am? An apology means nothing unless it's heard, Jeff."

Jeff stared at her and said nothing. His right eye twitched. He shook his head in uncertainty. The house creaked around them and the clock ticked. Chloe sighed. Jeff felt relief explode from her like a dam broken. He pushed the soup away and set back in his chair, searching her face for an answer. Chloe rose and moistened a washcloth she had retrieved from a cabinet. The house was silent around them, the silence of the darkening night. Not even the wind blew outside.

"We should get some rest," she said, placing the damp cloth on his forehead. He hadn't realized how much he missed being touched. He closed his eyes and let the sensation in.

Jeff swallowed. He needed to tell her the truth. He scratched at his raw forearm. "I hear this voice." He did not look at her when he said this. "I know you've heard it too. At first I thought it was…. It doesn't matter. But now it feels like it's inside me. Like whatever is here…."

She grabbed his hand. "Let's get out of here, Jeff. Let's move. It was a bad idea to come here in the first place. I admit it and take full responsibility for all of this."

"Can we do that? Just up and move?"

Chloe offered an uncertain and frightened smile. It shook like a leaf clinging to a tree in a storm. "We'll just sell. We'll put it up on the Internet. Somebody will see it. In the meantime, we can stay with family. What do you say?"

"Not your parents."

"Ethan, then. We can stay with Ethan. He'd be happy to have us."

For once he was compliant. He gave her the reins but said nothing more about the subject.

"Let's go to bed," she said, still holding his hand and pulling him up.

His hand went to her face and he touched her cheek gently. "Not just yet," he said. "Soon, but not tonight. I'm not ready."

She seemed to lose air. "I understand," she said as she let go of his hand and slowly walked to the bedroom.

The power faded again as he watched her walk away. He expected her to turn around and plead with him to come to bed, but that did not happen. The couch awaited him.

GHOST OF A MAD DOG

CHLOE DROVE a couple of hours out of her way to avoid shopping in Wicker. It wasn't that she had anything against the quality of merchandise in town. All the shops were stocked with the best foods for winter storms. She took issue with the people. She knew she would get stares, both judging and stupefied, from those in town who had heard, or had possibly been on the receiving end, of Lana's arms rage. Chloe wanted to avoid that conversation as long as possible. The fact was, she now thought everyone who climbed Bad Luck Hill to get a peek at the actress deserved whatever they got. The one consolation about her eventual trip back into Wicker for shopping would be the absence of nosy Odette. Her sister Alma didn't talk at all, it seemed, and so Chloe would be able to get in and out of their store without a problem.

Chloe was so excited for a fresh start with Jeff—until yesterday the man she had felt a growing dislike for with each passing hour—that she didn't mind the drive out of Wicker. She imagined the townsfolk with their mouths agape as she passed them by. "What about us?" they said in her imaginings. "Come shop with us. Tell us your secrets. Let us pry."

"No," she was saying with a condescending half grin as she sat proudly with both hands on the steering wheel. "Fuck off."

She had slept well the night before. She wished Jeff had come to bed with her, but that would take time. Sooner or later, they would curl up like kittens, like they did when they were first dating. Like they did when they had led an adventure tour through the Rocky Mountains. They had cuddled and curled then too. They had also purred. The memory of him around her was what had gotten her to sleep last night.

And yet… there was still that resentment in the air of the cottage. It slept with them both. Chloe knew the faces of certain invisible things. These things had no real form and only scientific definitions. Oxygen. Regret. Rage. These things were more like encompassments. They surrounded everyone all the time. Love looked like sunshine through a cracked window. Death looked like the dark in a hospital room the night before brain surgery. Resentment was the midnight glowering in the bedroom of a cabin in the woods.

Chloe found a grocery store and pharmacy in a town called Ready. Inside, it was a frenzy of people hoarding for the storm. To her relief, none of them paid much attention to her. None of them knew a thing about her, nor did they care to. She filled her shopping cart with cans of soup and boxes of cereal. She avoided meats. They would spoil if the power went off for any long periods of time. She got some cold medicine for Jeff and remembered to get food for Lana as well, though the actress had not asked it of her. Chloe imagined somewhere in the big house there was a great storage room of food that fed the actress well.

She was inspecting a bottle of blackberry wine—not a necessity, but a nicety—when her cell phone buzzed. Ethan. He was one of the few she had given the new number to and the only one who had yet used it.

"How's Jeff?" he said. Not a word of hello. He was brisk, and the words came like a slap over the phone. "Hello, Ethan. Jeff is fine. He's still sick. I'm at the store getting him some meds and stocking up for the storm heading our way." She had the aisle to herself. There weren't many people interested in purchasing liquor when a blizzard was bearing down on them.

"Do you have enough food?" There was that accusatory edge to his voice again. As if Chloe couldn't possibly take care of Jeff. She was surprised by the clarity with which that tone came through, but then remembered she was no longer on Bad Luck Hill. There was reception in Ready.

"That's why I'm here at the grocery store, Ethan," she said, throwing her own edge into the conversation. She put the wine in the cart and wheeled it up to the register. There was a line, but not as long as she had expected.

"I meant to call the other day but got busy with school. I heard about Lana and her rifle. Shooting at a chopper? There will be charges. Not exactly the safest neighbor, is she?"

"There are no safe neighbors." She realized she believed this. And aside from that, she felt protective of her new crazy Hollywood friend. "I think we're all one slipped phrase away from going postal."

There was silence on the line. The woman in front of her looked over her shoulder nervously.

"Listen, Ethan, I've got to go. I'm at the register." There were five carts ahead of her. "Jeff and I are planning on selling the cottage and moving back. Do you think you could put us up? It would just be for a bit until we find someplace new."

"Really? That's—"

"I'll get hold of you. It will probably be in the spring. It would be silly to talk of moving anywhere in this type of weather." She was hoping for sooner, but she didn't want to tell Ethan that. "Good-bye, Ethan."

If she could manage to convince Jeff to move right after the storm was over, they could find a nice cheap hotel to stay at until the cottage sold. Maybe they wouldn't need Ethan's help. It wouldn't even have to be a nice hotel. Being in their line of work, they had slept with worse things than hissing cockroaches.

Waiting there behind a woman who had taken every last loaf of bread on the shelves, Chloe had the sudden desire to hurry back home. Jeff was lying there on the couch sick. A nauseous anxiety made her dizzy. The ridiculous but not-so-silly "feeling" that Jeff was not alone in the cottage made her breathe a little faster. Something else was there, and it was most likely watching him. Digging into him. She tapped the back of her ring finger on the shopping cart handle. The line had to move faster. She had to get home now.

THE ROAD up Bad Luck Hill seemed steeper than usual. The winds pushed against the Jeep with greater intensity. Something, Chloe felt, was trying to keep her from Jeff. From their happy ending, much deserved. She always leapt to the most irrational of thoughts when threatened. She could hear her mother's voice telling her "Stop being silly, girl." And yet she felt the eyes around her. The shadows. Their gaze was intrusive, as if she were being studied or filmed. She just wanted to get back to the cottage. Everything had taken longer than expected. The checkout. The drive home. It was already dark.

When at last she reached the cottage, she sat in the Jeep for a moment, telling herself to move but unable to do so. The cottage seemed such an earnest place. So polite and welcoming. But it was a trap. The little insignificant place was chewing her and Jeff up. Her unease grew as she sat there. She gripped tight to the steering wheel, and her breath came short and fast again. The darkness around the cottage was pushing inward at the light inside. Pouring in through the windows, Chloe saw there were strange forms—distorted as if in a funhouse mirror—seeping inside with it. She blinked and wiped her eyes.

Finally, she pushed herself from the steering wheel and rushed to the cottage door. If there was something seeping in the air around her, she did not try to see it. Inside, though dimly lit by the burning wood in the fireplace, Jeff lay asleep on the couch, balled up beneath a blanket. He stirred at her entrance but did not wake. She felt his forehead. Still sick and getting worse. She should call the doctor in Wicker before the storm arrived and cut them off from civilization. But would Jeff even go into town to see him? He had a stubborn streak like an oil slick.

Chloe looked around the room. There was a rattling going on. The lamp beside the television tremored as if it had been bumped into, but only slightly. The floors creaked.

She unpacked the Jeep of the groceries, put them in the kitchen, and then returned to the center of the front room. She gave a slow, watchful turn. A full circle.

"I feel you," she whispered. Then, much louder and into the air, she said, "I'll be back, Jeff. I have to take some things to Lana. Then we're calling a doctor. I'll be right back."

She paused.

"Do you hear me?" This time she was not speaking to Jeff. "I'll be right back."

She heard a creak from the old rocker and looked in time to see it tip the tiniest bit forward. To let her know whatever it was, it would be waiting for her. She felt anger more than fear at that moment.

"I'll be right back."

CHLOE HAD planned to quickly drop the groceries off and then head back to be at Jeff's side. Lana showed her to the kitchen and Chloe brought the bags in and set them on the large center table, above which hung unused pots and pans. The kitchen was large and spacious, with utilities only a bit newer than those in the cottage. There was a large pantry opposite the doorway that Chloe could only guess stored piles of perishables.

Lana had never been a conversationalist and hadn't really encouraged Chloe to be one either. She just seemed to require occasional companionship. But this time, Chloe saw a more anticipatory gleam in the actress's eyes.

"Jeff's very ill," Chloe answered the unspoken plea. "I have to get back to him."

"I think your husband is fighting for his life," Lana said bluntly.

That gave Chloe pause, Lana's intended effect. She stood motionless in the middle of the kitchen, searching behind the meaning of the words. At last, she gathered herself and made her way to the front door without saying a thing. She opened the door to leave and could hear Lana bustling up behind her.

"He's in danger. And so are you. We all are."

"What do you mean?" Chloe asked, still in the doorway. The cold air blew in around her.

"When your husband pulled Michael's body up from the earth, I understood that my instinct to keep away from the cottage had been right all along. You felt it too. The recoiling. Like there is something crouched in the corners of that place."

Chloe shivered, though not from the cold. "Yes. I've felt it. Since the day we came here."

Lana turned to her library. "Follow me."

Chloe re-entered and shut the door behind her. "But I need to get back to Jeff."

Lana faced her. "And do what exactly? You can't do anything unless you know what you're up against."

"Do you know what we're up against?"

"No. But I'm searching."

Lana opened the library door. The room was lit by candles even though the power had not failed that night. There were candles on bookshelves, tables, and desks. On the center table, there were five candles burning in a half circle around the large leather volume that held such prominence in Lana's collection.

Lana gestured for Chloe to sit. "I need your help," Lana said. "And you need mine."

Chloe hesitated but eventually complied as Lana sat opposite her. "What are we doing?" Chloe asked.

"Research. Answers for us both, hopefully."

"I—I don't know about...."

Lana held up her hand to silence Chloe. She gripped the edges of the table and began to hum. Coming from the stoic actress and seemingly no-nonsense woman, anything melodic sounded abnormal and a bit disturbing. In the moment, Chloe noticed, to her relief, that the darkness around her did not seem polluted with spiritual debris as it did now at the cottage. There were no malformed shapes hiding in these corners. No. Those remained down the hill. With Jeff.

The thought of her husband made her want to go to him again, and she nearly rose to do so when Lana, in as commanding a voice as she had spoken, said, "Come out of the dark, come out of the past, come out of the corners, those who lived here last."

A séance! Chloe's eyes widened. She was calling forth spirits!

Chloe, stricken with fear, rose at once. "No! Lana, we shouldn't do this!"

"Hush, child! She comes!"

"She? Who? Who's coming?" She trembled and chased shadows with her eyes.

In the flicker of the candlelight, Lana's eyes fixed on Chloe.

"Who comes?" Chloe repeated.

"A mother," Lana whispered. "She will speak through another's tongue."

"You're going to let a spirit possess you?"

"No, my dear." Her voice expressed apology. "She will possess you."

Chloe's blood turned to ice, and she felt an unbearable itch beneath her skin that she could not scratch. She was pulled off her feet and out of her skin, then stuffed back in so far down she couldn't react. It immobilized her and forced her to collapse back into her seat. She could but let out a whine in protest. What occurred next Chloe saw as if she were watching a film. A film starring Lana Pruitt and an unknown, faceless woman. The victim. They conversed in the dark.

"Who are you?" Lana asked.

Out of Chloe's depths climbed the answer like a drunken climber, as if she was learning to speak after a stroke. The tongue wagged and was heavy, but the words were still understandable.

"I am his mother. He has me trapped."

There were bitterness and sadness to this mother. Chloe felt every bit of it, and it made her eyes roll to the back of her head.

"Whose mother are you?"

"He's a rascal." The mother looked around her. "Where am I? What am I doing here? This is not my cottage."

"I'm confused. Who is the rascal?"

"He is my boy. I tried to stop him. I tried to save him. To keep him. But always he tried to get away. Just like his father. His father I was able to see off on my terms, but…. If I had known… if I had known what the starving would cause…."

The mother noticed the book and screeched.

The mother began to wail, causing the house to shake. Lana stiffened in her chair.

"I thought I could starve the devil out! Starve him out! Starve him out!"

The mother beat at Chloe's form with limp appendages. "You must put me back, and you must all die. It's the only way to be sure." Lana stood at once and searched her book for what she should do.

"Stop!" Lana screamed. "Stop it!"

"This one is open," the mother said. "She's open and she has to die!"

The mother continued with her flagellation of Chloe's body. Chloe, deep inside her own being, felt the beating and began to force her way out of the haze. She climbed up until she could feel her own voice once again. The film she was watching flashed bright, and she felt her own mind push back through. Finally, it was she who was now screaming in the chair, clinging to its armrests. She inhaled deeply, as if she had been holding her breath for an extended period of time. Lana stood across from her against a bookshelf, her face a hideous mask of terror, even in the darkness, pale and regretful.

Chloe stood and stumbled. "Did you get what you wanted?" she screamed. "You fucking crazy bitch! Did you get what you needed?"

"I had to try. For both of us. Now I know. But there are other ways—"

"Fuck you! Keep away from me, you psychotic cunt!" She made her way to the front door, seizing at the walls. Her legs were coming back slowly and the itching had nearly dissipated. Lana followed her with trepidation.

"I'll keep looking. We both have to keep looking. It's what we must do."

"Try looking into your own soul rather than raping someone else's." Tears burned down Chloe's cheeks. Lana stood at the door, holding her hand out as if to pull Chloe back. To embrace her. But Chloe fumbled down the steps.

Chloe climbed into the Jeep and momentarily broke into raging sobs at the wheel. This was what she and Jeff were up against: some crazed ghost mother and her son. And to top it off, a crazed actress playing Glinda the Good Witch on the hill.

She pulled herself together and backed away from the big house. Lana stood in the doorway, her arm still stretched out and her pain as dark and apparent as her silhouette.

JEFF WAS faintly aware that Chloe was there. And then she wasn't. She had said something about taking groceries to Lana Pruitt. He had fallen in and out of consciousness so much during those minutes—barely twenty, but stretched by restless sleep—that he couldn't be certain of anything that had actually transpired. The only relief he felt from his illness was that the intolerable itching had seemed to stop, if briefly.

He heard the creak of the rocking chair and opened his eyes. There sat a boy, or what remained of one. If Jeff had his wits about him, if they were not being suppressed by the illness, he would certainly have jumped up in surprise. As it was, however, he lay there and examined the smiling figure. There was something familiar about him. Like Jeff had seen him before. His eyes were large and round, protruding from their sockets like a victim of starvation. Yet the smile was continuous, as if the facial muscles had frozen just so, exposing two rows of yellowed, crooked teeth, some broken, some missing. The boy wore only a dirty pair of white underwear. His skin was stretched so tightly across his rib cage as to be transparent. A broad floppy hat rested on one knee. His hair was bushy and unkempt. He simply stared at Jeff with those eyes. Unblinking. Smiling.

"Who are you?" Jeff mumbled. He wondered if he could even be heard.

"Me?" the young voice said with a recognizable giggle. "I'm the ghost of a mad dog."

"A ghost? You're the one that's been keeping us awake."

Another giggle. It made Jeff the tiniest bit more aware of his situation. He grew a trifle apprehensive and struggled to sit up. The cottage seemed to move around him. It too was uneasy.

"You're a ghost now. Fine. Who were you then?"

"I was just a boy looking to leave here at first. But Momma wouldn't let me. She'd a killt me first, like she did Daddy. I don't know if she tied me up in the barn to keep me from runnin' or to keep me from killing my brother."

"Jesus."

"That's what she thought." The ghost giggled and slapped his be-hatted knee. "She thought she could starve the devil out of me. Bring me to Jesus. But there ain't no devil. The position is open for the filling. You find that out soon enough when you die or get killt. There's only want. And I had a lot of want. You'd be surprised what you'll eat to stay alive. Any little rodent. Any little rock. I gnawed off a finger after two weeks. Momma went all hysterical when she saw what I done to myself. She untied me, and that was stupid of her. I knocked her down and I ran out the barn door. I forgot all about the well."

"You fell down the well...."

"I fell down the well, Mister. You better believe it. I got my finger back, though." He wiggled an index finger on a skinny, dirty little hand. Smiling. Eyes blazing. "I sure do miss eating. The want didn't go away after I fell. I'm hungry all the dang time."

"What happened to your momma?"

"Oh, she got a book, did some hocus-pocus thing thinking she could stop me getting what I want. Didn't work, though. Now she's the one that's trapped."

Jeff watched as the boy went into a fit of giggles. The cottage expanded and whined around him.

"And what is it that you want?" Jeff asked his fever dream.

The ghost rose from the rocking chair. It only moved a little at his rising, as if merely touched by the wind. He walked barefoot across the room. Oddly, the floor creaked under the weight of the ghost.

"Before I can get what I want, I need something from you, Mister."

Jeff kept his tired eyes on this strange apparition. This rascal. He watched it lazily put the hat back on its head.

"What?"

"I need you to let me in," said the large-eyed ghost with an oblique stare.

Jeff felt the itch start up again. All over. An irritating invasion and molestation.

"Why?"

"Because I want your teeth."

The smile full of useless teeth menaced at Jeff from beneath the rim of the hat. Jeff's stomach acid surged and he spit up on the floor. The ghost boy flicked his tongue like a snake, as if he wanted to lick up the bile.

Jeff did not want to ask why the ghost desired his teeth. He just understood he had to fight. The sick feeling in his gut was growing until it felt like he would shit his pants and vomit at the same time. All he could do was deny the rascal's want with what power he had.

"Damn," the rascal said. "You're a stubborn son of a bitch."

The ghost boy glanced at the baseball bat in the corner of the room, then back at Jeff. His teeth glowed and were all Jeff could see of the boy's face. "I'll get in somehow, sonny boy. You can bet the farm on that."

THE TEMPERATURE had begun steadily dropping and the winds had picked up when Chloe parked the Jeep outside the cottage. Her visit with Lana had been terrifying. She had no idea how far the woman would go to be with her daughter, but she'd never expected a psychic assault. She turned off the ignition and sat at the wheel. The winds rocked the Jeep, tempting her to get out, but she remained there for some time, dazed and trembling. She wiped her face and nose with her hand. She knew Lana was still watching in the direction of the cottage, even if she could not see her. Chloe's rage was murderous, a hot bottle ready to explode.

Finally, she got out of the Jeep and went into the cottage. It was completely dark. The power had gone out and the fire was but embers. Through the sparse light offered by the night, she saw Jeff lying, a crumpled heap, on the floor in front of the couch. He moaned and squirmed, grabbing at his stomach. She ran to his side and instinctively reached for her cell phone.

"Please let there be reception!" she said. Jeff moved. "Jeff, honey. We're going to go to the hospital. We're getting out of here right now. Hang on!"

"No." He groaned. "No doctor. I don't need one. It's only…."

No reception. "Fuck!"

"The rascal. It's only…."

"I'll be right back," Chloe said. The phrase was an echo from her promise earlier that night. "I'm going to start the Jeep."

At least, she thought, she could get him out of the cottage. Away from all this sudden rush of madness.

She left the cottage door open as she ran to the Jeep. She turned the key, but there was nothing. The battery was gone. The cold had sapped it of its power. The Jeep hadn't even a last cough to give her. She tried again and again, but nothing still.

"Fuck!" She held her hands to her face. "Think. What to do."

Then she heard it. A giggle. Not with her in the Jeep, but from the cottage door and carried on the wind. It was with her husband. The door slammed shut, separating her from Jeff.

Chloe sprinted back and pulled at the knob, but it did not give. "Keep away from him!" she screamed. She banged on the glass. "Jeff! Wake up. Let me in."

Distorted forms danced in her periphery. The fiddler played in the woods.

With as much strength as she could muster and as solid a force as could be reckoned, she pushed against the door and it gave. She rushed into the cottage, staring around, on guard. Jeff was still where she had found him, doubled over on the floor.

"You keep away from him," she warned the air.

Quickly, she crawled beside Jeff and reached for her cell phone again. There still wasn't any reception and there might not be for a while. The storm was there and had arrived as angry as she had ever seen one. But there might just be enough power to get a text message through. She brought up Ethan on her address list.

HELP. COME NOW.

It sent. Now she could only wait and fend off whatever force haunted the cottage. Whatever unseen thing watched them.

Two Brothers

ETHAN WAS not a racer. Even as a child he avoided the go-cart races on the block, the ones that helped solidify Jeff as the resident Golden Boy. But he was racing now. In his respectable blue Alero, he made turns with the skill of a getaway artist. It was Ethan against the elements. He had to get out of town before the storm made its way over land and iced the roads impassable. By the weather reports, he knew the worst of it had already reached Jeff and Chloe and that his drive there would only get more treacherous. He tried not to think on that, however. He listened to the calming voice of the GPS system and did exactly as he was instructed, having entered the address to the cottage from the mass e-mail from Chloe he had received and saved months ago.

It had already been dark when Ethan's phone lit up beside him on the desk back home. Chloe texted a plea through the distance and at once he stopped going over his lesson plans on the computer. She might as well have been standing right beside him, screaming. He jumped in his seat. He tried to return a message, then a call, but nothing went through.

"Storm of the century." He had been hearing the phrase all week, as if the apocalypse was nigh. People were hoarding hysterically. Meteorologists were screaming as usual, but this time, it seemed, for good reason. And here he was, having to drive through all of it. Something had happened to Jeff. Ethan rattled with anxiety. He was going to have to leave his neat, warm life for something much chillier than a winter blizzard.

He began packing at once, filling a duffel bag he had kept since college with whatever clothes he happened to come across.

It was a desperate and mindless forage through the house. Kelton, holding the sleeping baby, watched with bemusement as Ethan leapt from room to room.

"What are you doing?" he whispered over the baby's head.

Ethan knew the look on Kelton's face. It was the same look from the night Ethan had threatened to leave him the year before Bug came into their lives. As if his whole face had fallen apart and was trying to piece itself back together.

"Something's happened to Jeff. I've got to go, Kel."

"There's a blizzard coming!" Too loud. Bug stirred. "There's a blizzard coming," he whispered again.

"He's my brother. Try and understand." He raced around, grabbing and packing.

"No. You're not going. Besides, what about your classes?"

"Look at the forecast. Do you actually think there will be school? The whole city will be a ghost town by tomorrow morning."

"Because people are smart. They avoid danger. You're wanting to run right into it like a mad buffalo. You're not supposed to tease danger, Ethan." He was face to face with Ethan now. The baby was awake and staring at the two of them in confusion.

"I have to go to him. He needs my help." Ethan swung the duffel bag over his shoulder. "It's family."

Kelton calmed himself. "You don't even talk to him anymore. They've cut you out of their lives. Chloe's made sure of that. We're your family now. Me and Bug."

Ethan kissed Kelton and then Bug. "And you mean more to me than I can say. But he's still my brother. I can't deny that. There are still ties, invisible and strained as they might be. They pull me, Kel. I have to go."

He gave Bug another hug and then walked to the door.

"Ethan," Kelton said. But there was nothing more to say. "You stubborn jackass. Be very careful."

"I'll call you when I get there."

"Say bye-bye to Daddy, Bug."

"Bye-bye."

Ethan had waited until he pulled out of the driveway before he let a single frightened tear escape. And now there he was, on strange highways with strange cars. The miles did not stretch, however. He heard nothing but the kindly GPS woman and his own inner fears. He focused on the road, which he found an easier task at night. He was only forced to slow down when the snow began to fall in thick clumps. The storm had met him, and it was hungry, eclipsing most of the northern coast.

By the time he reached Wicker, he was crawling. He had stopped briefly a few times for gas and coffee, but didn't linger too long in any location. He had not beaten the storm, but he had seen the bully eye to eye.

Wicker resembled a nuclear testing site: all the buildings were perfect and livable, yet there seemed to be no life in the town at all, only snow and dark windows. The faintest hint of candles and lamps could be seen through them if he looked closely, but there was not a soul to be seen. The shop windows watched the Alero eke past.

The hill was farther still, and Ethan feared the car might not make it. It was a daunting climb, and that was before he had even crossed the creek. Branches burdened by snow scratched the car roof, sending a chill through him. Whatever it is, don't let it in.

It was at the creek that the car finally could not take it anymore and died. He felt a tilt as it climbed over a slant, and then there was silence. He tried to start the car again, cursing at it, but even harsh language did not convince the vehicle to continue the steep ascent. Ethan looked ahead and up the hill, still holding tight to the steering wheel until his hands turned white. There was one of two things he could now do. He either had to get up to the top of that hill or freeze to death in the car.

He tried calling Kelton, but there was no service. Frustrated, he reached for his duffel bag in the passenger's seat and the flashlight in the glove compartment and then carefully climbed from the tilted car and onto the coated rocks of the creek. A cold blast of wind shocked him and he nearly fell straight away.

"Just get there, Ethan," he comforted himself. "Things aren't as bad as they seem." The hill and every tree on it watched him.

He followed the road through the trees by foot. The snow wasn't as deep there, having been deflected by the branches. Despite the occasional fall, he made good time. He kept the flashlight focused on the ground in front of him. Ethan did not care to see what, if any, eyes glared at him in the night. If there were a hungry wolf or bear in the woods, he would have no chance against them anyway. There was one goal and that was to get to the cottage.

There came a point that he knew he was being followed. He heard the slight crunch of snow underfoot, and it did not pair with his own. His heart began to speed, and his breath quickened. The darkness squeezed at him like a too-tight blanket. Ahead, the trees lessened in density. If he could get there, he would be fine. He began to walk faster. But the tread behind him was quickening as well, until he was certain he could hear breathing, even feel it on his neck.

He lost the argument with his fear and looked over his shoulder. It took him a moment to realize what he was seeing. Near him—too near—was the burly outline of another, and much larger, human form. It moved suddenly toward him. He was startled and lost his footing. His cheek smacked the snow, and he gave a muffled cry. With little to stop him, his body slid back on the ice-slide road toward the figure. He was panicked now. So much so that when he finally came to a stop, he could not get himself to open his eyes, afraid of what he might see. Yet when he finally did, there was nothing to be seen. He looked around. No burly form anywhere. Just the bitter cold quiet of the night and the icy echo of the snow.

His flashlight, which he had dropped in his terror, lay a few feet in front of him. He quickly rose and grabbed it. He stumbled more now, making up lost ground, than he had on the entire climb up the hill. Soon, however, he was out of the dense woods, and he saw hope.

The big house was in view before he came upon the cottage. It was a massive silhouette against the sky, hardly discernible through the dark and the falling snow. Everything was blurred. Ethan wiped the flakes from his eyelashes.

Soon the trees to the cliff petered out and made way for a long drop to one side. Ethan walked closer to the woods, wary of another slip in the snow and a fall from the cliff. Ahead of him, he saw the old Jeep their father had given to Jeff. It was covered in snow, and the little cottage looked dark and lifeless. From inside he saw movement. Light, at least. He found himself calling out before he had even reached the porch.

"Jeff! Chloe!"

The scene inside the cottage was confusing at first. Ethan burst through the door with a flurry of flakes to find Jeff lying on the floor under a thick sleeping bag and a blanket. He did not move at the sudden noise. Chloe sat beside him, wrapped in a bed cover. Logs burned in the fireplace, providing the glow Ethan had seen from outside. The rest of the cottage was dark, as if the world ended outside of the fire's light. The shadows were large on the world's edges. Yet the sense Ethan had—that of being watched—returned once more. It had vanished after his fall in the woods to be replaced by naked panic.

"What are you doing on the floor? Get him on the couch." Ethan rushed to his brother's side. Jeff was shivering and unconscious.

Chloe looked at Ethan with an expression she had never given him before: hope. "He fell. I couldn't lift him back up. Help me?"

Jeff groaned a little as the two positioned him back on the couch. An arm slipped out from the sleeping bag, and Ethan saw the long, jagged scratch marks on Jeff's forearm and then corresponding marks on his face and neck. They looked deep and scarring. Ethan looked to Chloe in horror and accusation.

"He won't stop. He itches all the time. I've even tried to wrap him, but he tears the bandages and tape right off."

"Maybe he's allergic to something."

"Maybe." Chloe sounded doubtful. From the ferocious look of the scratches, so was Ethan. These were not the scratch marks to quell some itch. These were excavations. Ethan began to think the source might be something more psychological.

"What happened here, Chloe? Tell me everything."

"You would not believe me, Ethan."

Ethan rolled his eyes in exasperation. "Is this more of your religious crap? Is that what you think this is all about? Some evil demon?"

"I've seen it," she hissed, her lips curling. "So has Jeff."

He held her gaze momentarily and tightened his jaw. "Okay, then," he finally said. "Tell me what happened. What boogeyman is haunting you now?"

"As long as you don't interrupt me with your stupid questions."

"Then I'm going to need something to drink."

"The liquor cabinet is in the kitchen." She pointed into the dark.

Ethan readied his flashlight.

"The kitchen floor squeaks something awful," Chloe said. "But don't worry. It's only a kitchen floor."

Under the covers, Jeff itched at his groin.

"We'll need to get something for his scratches as well," Ethan said. "Some Neosporin. Where's the bathroom? I'm not afraid of the dark."

THE SNOW stopped falling just before dawn. Ethan was drawn to the breaking light at the window. The world outside had been erased, and all that remained was something bleak and bare. Shades of white, gray, and blue met the shrouded sun as it rose over the sea.

Ethan had listened to Chloe tell what she knew. Or what she thought she knew. Ethan was now more convinced than ever that she had something to do with all of this. He no longer thought she was an outright bitch. He thought she was insane, maybe having experienced one too many falls from mountaintops.

She was silent behind him, perhaps waiting for a response. But what could he give her but applause at a tale well told? And it was a good tale. She had delivered it with earnestness. A+ for effort. He knew now she thought it was true. But there were no such things as ghosts. At least, not the kind to which she was referring. There were many dangerous invisible things in the world. Things that needed warning signs. But what was dead was dead.

Ethan watched as the wind whipped the snow into the air. He could almost make out figures in the chaos. Patterns in the morning light. Patterns everywhere. The human eye loved patterns. They were easy to understand and relay. Jeff was part of Ethan's life pattern. It was always all about Jeff.

When they were kids and Jeff came down with the flu, the world might as well have stopped. Ethan was on the outside looking in as his father and mother tended to the Golden Boy. They fussed over him ridiculously. Ethan was only let in to see his brother when they needed a washcloth or cough medicine. And here he was again—on the outside as Chloe tended to Jeff on the couch. Ethan looked at her as she combed back the hair from Jeff's damp forehead.

"The sun is up. We should try to get him to a real hospital. I don't trust small-town doctors."

"Where's your car?" Chloe asked.

"At the bottom of the hill. It didn't make it past the creek." He walked over and sat in the rocking chair.

"You walked up the hill?"

"Of course." He was shocked that she was shocked. "He's my brother. Why do I keep having to remind people of that fact? No. We didn't talk, but dammit, he was my brother."

"I stand chided," she said. She fixed Jeff's covers and sat against the couch on the floor. "So, what do we do?"

"Dig out the Jeep."

"No good." She shook her head. "It's not starting. I think it's finally died for good."

"Shit." Ethan hit the arms of the chair. He thought for a moment, chewing on his fingernails. "We could try to get my car started again. Last night I just wanted to get up here as quickly as possible. I didn't spend too long at the ignition. If we could get it going, then we could drive into that little town and get some help."

"There's little alternative, is there?"

"Whatever illness he has, it's wrecking him. We can't wait for someone to climb the hill and find us."

"It's not an illness. It's—"

"Let's just get him out of here, okay? We can talk about all of this later."

Jeff turned in his sleep and let out a long, cold whimper. Chloe's hand went to her throat.

"Whatever we do, we need to do it now." Frozen, Ethan sat in the chair, the whimper temporarily having destroyed any resentment he still held toward his brother.

There was a brief moment when neither of them moved. They played a waiting game. Who would volunteer to leave Jeff's side? Chivalry had no place in the cottage, and though she had hated every second of it, Chloe had hiked through a blizzard or two in her travels.

"You go," Ethan finally said. "I'd like to spend some time with him."

Chloe stood and let her blanket fall from her shoulders. "Keep him warm and stay close. Having someone near him seems to keep away…. It seems to calm him."

She went to the bedroom and layered herself. She did not plan to be out in the cold for very long, but her career—and her life—had taught her to always prepare for bitter surprises.

Ethan tossed her the keys as she headed out the door. He did not rise from the chair. Chloe gave one last look at Jeff and then quickly left, making sure as little cold air as possible was let into the cottage.

Ethan watched Jeff, who trembled miserably beneath the coverings. "Well, Brother," Ethan said. "It's you and me. And I haven't the first idea as to what to do."

He decided to see to the washrag that lay across his brother's forehead. After that, he tried to get Jeff to take a drink of water, sitting him up so that he would not choke and stroking Jeff's throat to relax it so that at least a gulp of water would be swallowed. This was a trick his mother had taught him in those brief episodes when Jeff's sheen was nowhere to be seen. Ethan was hesitant to admit it, but when he was growing up, he looked forward to the days when Jeff was gone to football camp or some such bravado-making institution. Ethan found that his mother paid him more attention then. She loved him, and he knew this, but she did not show it the way she did with Jeff. Jeff sucked up every ounce of attention. Ethan ground his teeth as the memories seeped back.

"We should probably talk, huh?" he said as he dabbed some of the deeper scratches on Jeff's face with Neosporin. "Or else I'm going to become a bitter alcoholic and Kel will divorce me."

He rose once Jeff showed no signs of waking, and took a walk around the cottage in the light. The kitchen, he found, did not look half as creepy as it sounded. In fact, it was rather quaint. Just very old. Old things complained not from pain, but from uselessness.

Ethan tried to call Kelton again. No service. Kelton was probably worried sick by now. He always thought too much. He worried too much. Like a good mother. Perhaps that was why Ethan fell for him: his caring, his gentleness. Ethan longed for that now, to be held in Kelton's arms. He regretted not spending just a few more moments in an embrace before he sped out the door for Wicker.

He noted the computer sitting idle on the kitchen table. Chloe's story had been absolutely beyond sane, but Ethan could not explain the image he had seen behind her when they had been chatting online. He looked at the kitchen doorway where the strange figure had stood. It was assuredly not Jeff, and after a few slight investigations of the cottage, he decided Chloe wasn't cheating again. So then, who was that? They hadn't made friends with any of the townsfolk. That was certain. They were very much alone there. And in fact, they seemed, by the tenor in Chloe's voice, to be rather miserable there as well. At least, Chloe did. The only company had been Lana Pruitt, and the image Ethan had seen on the computer screen was certainly not that of a faded film star.

And then there was something else about Chloe, altogether more personal, that bothered Ethan. When she was telling him what had happened and she spoke of her "feelings," her premonitions, it had made him very angry. It had been her premonitions, after all, that had nearly cost him and Kelton the adoption of Bug. Sure, the bridge had collapsed, but coincidence did not excuse bigotry.

Yet Ethan wondered....

His own "feelings" that something was wrong, that something terrible was happening to Jeff, they had seemingly been accurate. What if these were along the same lines as Chloe's own premonitions?

"We're all psychic in some way," she had once said at a dinner when Jeff first introduced her to Ethan and Kelton. They were at a bar and grill in the middle of a shopping plaza. Jeff had seemed uncomfortable with the subject, looking around as if waiting for the opportunity to excuse his wife's quirks. But what if she was right? What if the entire planet was like a big ball of string, everything truly connected to everything else, like some New Ager's dream?

Ethan shook his head at the thought. Proof. That's what he relied on. Things that could be broken or bruised, mended and embraced. Prove to him that a ghost exists and then maybe he'd believe it. At the moment, however, the solid world was causing quite enough problems without adding the invisible to the mix.

The sound of Jeff's voice brought Ethan back to the couch. Jeff mumbled and groaned. With wide strides, Ethan was at his brother's side in no time. But Jeff lay still and undisturbed.

"Pull out of it," Ethan said. "Mom's the resident vegetable of our family."

He felt Jeff's forehead again, then sighed and looked around the room. His eyes rested on a baseball bat against the wall.

"God, I hated baseball." He spoke to battle the silence, which was becoming increasingly unbearable. "I mean, I hated all sports, but especially baseball. Maybe because Dad expected me to like it so much. But I wasn't you, and he wanted a whole yard full of Jeffs."

Jeff moaned and turned his face to the back of the couch. Ethan picked up the bat and studied it.

"Do you remember when he decided he was going to teach me baseball if it killed him? He dragged me outside and made me play, thinking me an idiot of the game. I knew the rules, though.

I had seen you play enough. But I wanted to see him frustrated. I wanted his face to explode in red. I think it was because that was the only time I ever got his full attention—when I pissed him off. That's what my inner psychiatrist tells me anyway. Well, finally, after an hour of me holding the bat intentionally fey, he got so fed up, he took it from me and he hit my shoulder with it." Ethan laughed. "The look on his face—the shock at what he had done mixed with rage—that was priceless. Completely worth the pain in my shoulder. And then when he turned around and saw that you had seen him hit me…. He never bothered me again after that. He never so much as talked to me. And you became my protector, though you didn't know it. God, I hated baseball."

How easy it would be, he thought, to swing. To bash his brother's head in. What poetic justice!

Ethan put the baseball bat back in the corner. He returned to the couch and adjusted Jeff's covers. Jeff's eyes twitched and raced beneath their lids. His skin was pale and broken. Ethan bent down and whispered in his brother's ear, "What are you thinking, Golden Boy? What are you thinking right now?"

JEFF'S FEVER dreams, like all hallucinations, incorporated some of the images and sounds happening around him. He lay on the couch, but he felt he was no longer in the cottage. Instead, he was in a hospital room so dull and white and clean he felt nauseated. Fluorescent lighting washed out everything, even the smallest hint of color. Blue was not blue. Red had no strength to be red.

People or staff came and went. Chloe was there at first as a nurse. Her voice was a far-off thing, sifted clean of emotion. Then, in some strange hallucinatory shift change, Ethan took over. They were both dressed in white uniforms, crisp and pressed. Jeff tried to say something more than once, but neither of his nurses heard him. They were only there to keep him alive. Not to converse.

And then, there was another. A voice whose speaker stood just outside of Jeff's periphery. He could not turn his head to see the speaker, but he recognized the shrill voice.

"They can't hear you, you know. There's only me. Invite me in."

But Jeff never would. He knew better. The voice continued plaguing him, stopping only when Ethan came back into the hospital room.

Someone sat at a computer in front of his bed, hen-pecking at the keys. The very large monitor obscured the typist's face. Behind the typist was a window that portrayed an endless orange-streaked sky and a dipping giant moon. The clouds in the sky rushed past the window at an incredible speed. Jeff accepted this the way any hallucinating person would: with the knowledge that one's surroundings are out of their control. That everything happening is perfectly rational.

He found that he could move. He looked around and saw another bed next to his. It took him a moment to realize who was lying in it.

"Mom!" he said. His voice traveled in a muted echo.

She looked at him with a bittersweet smile, a smile so missed, though Jeff could sense the worry etched in the lines of her face. He rose with ease and went to her, taking her hand.

"Mom. You're awake!" He squeezed her hand and started to cry. She had been in dreams before, but not like this. Not this real. This must be true!

Her hand squeezed back. Her hair was long again, not cut short as it had been in the care facility. It flowed in a beautiful white stream down her thin shoulders, shoulders he knew could carry more than he could ever imagine.

"No." She shook her head sadly. "You're asleep, hon. And I'm just visiting."

He was certain his face had fallen because his mother patted his hand. "There now," she said. "No time for that. You've got to leave this place. Both the dream and the cottage. Take Ethan and go."

"How did you know about the cottage?"

"I'm just visiting. You need to wake up, Jeffrey. You need to get away from him." She turned as serious as he had ever seen her. Her face was set in stone. "The one who comes in here and tempts you. I hear him whispering at you. You need to get away from him. Don't let him in, whatever you do."

"I won't. I mean, I'm trying not to. But it's been so hard."

"No excuses!" She seemed angry now. "Get away, Jeffrey. Wake up now!"

A loud clearing of the throat came from the typist.

"And stay away from him as well." Her eyes were aimed like missiles at the computer.

Jeff looked over his shoulder. "Who?"

"Your father. He means to—"

"Dad?"

Before he knew what he was doing or, for that matter, had any choice in the direction his dream was taking him, he found himself drawing closer to the typist. He looked back to see his mother, but she and her bed had vanished, replaced by a void. The typist came more fully into view, and the familiar angles of his father's face appeared. The old man (for he had always looked old as long as Jeff could remember) looked up at Jeff, though his fingers still attacked the keyboard with zeal. The sky behind him had turned ominous, but no less urgent. Instead of orange clouds racing by, there were beaten clouds of black and dark blue.

The old man did not seem the stern father he had once been. The crags and the cliffs were still evident on his face, but they no longer seemed as dangerous.

Jeff grinned. "Dad!"

Tap tap tap. Relentless.

"Dad, it's me. It's Jeff."

Nothing but the focused stare and the tapping on the keyboard. A tapping that grew even more frenzied.

Jeff moved over to his father's side of the desk. The typing suddenly stopped and his father sat motionless, his head still facing the monitor but his hands now dead on his lap.

"Forgive me," the old man said. His voice was weak and sullen.

He rose and offered Jeff his seat in front of the computer. He refused to look at Jeff as they changed positions, staring down at the floor, his arms hanging limply at his sides now.

Bewildered, Jeff took the seat offered him. The monitor held a pattern, one sentence written continuously.

I HAVE TO KILL YOU I HAVE TO KILL YOU

Jeff looked back at his father, who was now crying. His face looked as if it had been bathed in water but not dried off. Jeff was horrified.

"I'm sorry," the old man said. "He wants you. He wants a place in your body, my son. But if you die, he won't have a place to stay. I have to kill you. You see that now, don't you? He would take you from me, and I can't allow that."

The dream lost all light. The computer went black. The sound of a fluorescent light struggling and flickering could be heard somewhere. The window let only the dark blues that raced in the sky shade the room. His father, who stood with his back to the window, was a threatening silhouette.

"I won't let him in, Dad," Jeff protested. "I won't let him in!"

Jeff suddenly felt like a child trying to avoid punishment.

"It's too late." His father's voice sounded distant. "There's nothing you can do. He's watching you. He's watching Chloe."

The blue light would not let Jeff see his father clearly. The computer monitor flicked back to life and Jeff turned to face it. He had barely read the words that filled the screen

AND I WON'T BE STOPPED

before he felt his father take hold of his chin and tip his head back. Sharpness was drawn across Jeff's throat as he looked into his father's eyes.

Jeff woke screaming in the cottage. Ethan rushed to his side. He held him, wiping away the sweat from Jeff's forehead as they both shook.

"It's a nightmare," Ethan comforted his brother. "It was just a nightmare. That's all. You're okay."

Ethan was there, Jeff thought. Ethan was really there. Jeff wanted to tell him how sick he was. He wanted to tell Ethan of the illness he had inherited.

"Ethan. He's trying to kill me!" Jeff said in the frantic, tired dialect of the terminally ill. He had never been, nor had he ever sounded, he was sure, more frightened.

"No, no, no. Shhh. It's a nightmare. No one is trying to harm you."

Jeff was not comforted. "Dad! Dad is trying to kill me. Help me, Ethan! Help me!"

Jeff held tight to his brother. He felt Ethan's arms tighten around him, trying to match his strength with desperate force. Jeff remembered Ethan playing baseball in the yard with their father. He remembered the moment he saw his father hit Ethan with the bat.

"He's trying to kill us, Ethan."

"Dad's been dead for years, Jeff. Shhh."

And they rocked together on the old couch, both in tears.

Miles away in a care facility that prided itself on its record of quick turnover, a now-empty room was being readied for a new resident. There were new bed linens and new flowers on order. The previous occupant had passed away during the night, a woman who had come to them with long silver hair.

LOST GIRL

THE COTTAGE was silent but for its now-incessant, nervous creaking. Jeff lay quiet again. Ethan had rocked him until the trauma had passed and he fell once more into a deep sleep. Ethan wrapped his brother up tight in the blanket and the sleeping bag and watched him from the kitchen doorway as he tried to call Kelton once more. He needed a comforting voice. A voice that he was certain loved him. But the weather and the hill was not letting him connect. Relationships, it seemed, in this age of advancement and breakthroughs depended on climate.

He tried calling again in the hopes that something would get through, even if it was only a single ring. But by his third attempt, he huffed in resignation and put the cell phone back in his pants pocket.

The creaking, especially in the kitchen, was turning into quite an annoyance. It was as if the house were crawling, shaking, and creeping its way right to the edge of the hill. The walls stretched and groaned like unused tendons and pummeled bones. The old place was whining and waiting to pitch itself off the cliff side.

Ethan walked to the kitchen sink and looked out the window at the red barn covered in snow. Every so often when a breeze would kick up, a large patch of snow would fall to the ground from tree limbs or the roofline. Ethan's eyelids grew heavy as he stood there, as if he had taken a sleeping aid and it was kicking in. Something pulled at him, a heavy warmth, lulling him like a brush through the hair. He felt covered by the sensation.

What he saw before him changed. Children were playing in the snow outside, as if they had simply strolled into his sightline. But that was impossible. There were no children around there.

This is a memory. Get to bed before you hurt yourself.

There were two boys in the snow, happy and unencumbered by thoughts of growing up. And there was a little girl too. Maybe a sister. Only Jeff and Ethan hadn't had a little sister. No matter. The memory played on. Snowballs were thrown and laughs were tossed. Laughing and… cackling. Jeff was cackling. Strange that Ethan had never remembered Jeff to cackle before. Not like that. But then, they had never really played together before. Not like that.

The moment paused. Jeff, the handsome boy he had been, stood tall in the snow and looked at Ethan in the kitchen window. The other two memories—little Ethan and the little girl—ran off to play in the woods, but Jeff stayed and beckoned Ethan out of the cottage with quick, curling finger gestures. Ethan smiled. It had been so long since he and Jeff had spent any real time together. When they were younger, once Jeff had turned to gold, Ethan became rust.

But now… now he wanted to play. How sweet! How wonderful!

CHLOE MADE it to Ethan's car. The inches of snow had allowed her good traction on the road for the most part. She had twice slipped because of the decline, but she reached the creek unscathed and unbruised. When she saw Ethan's car sitting on its slant, she breathed a sigh of relief. At that moment, it was the most beautiful vehicle she had ever seen. Though heavy clouds still hung in the sky, to her eyes there might as well have been a silver halo surrounding the wreck. She could get it started. She chanted that intent to herself in a mantra. Ethan just hadn't tried. He had said so himself.

She cautiously climbed over the loose and shaky rocks of the creek to the other side where the car sat idle. The creek slabs looked like cold razors. Her heart skipped a few beats at misplaced footsteps, but she reached the door of the car with no problem. She wiped away the snow from the windows, the hood, and the roof. Once she got in the Alero and got it started, she didn't want to have to get back out to clean the thing off. She pulled at the door handle, the cold digging into her gloveless fingers, biting them numb. Why was everything so cold in her life? Where was the warmth? Where was the fucking warmth?

Eventually, just as she was thinking she might need to smash a window, the door gave. She jerked back from the force of her pulling, a bit disappointed she was not going to be able to shatter something and get away with it. She got in the car.

Chloe's attempts at starting the car proved just as futile as Ethan's. Her fingers began to bleed with the twisting of the keys in the cold. The car gave a few gurgles and teases, but nothing came of them. Chloe hit the dashboard and screamed in frustration, the breath in front of her face making a frenzied design. Her eyes were tearing up, but this was not the time for hysterics.

As she gripped the steering wheel, trying to think of something rational and useful, trying to think of anything to keep from having to go back up the hill, she caught movement in the rearview mirror. She took in a sharp breath and froze. Something had dodged into the trees behind the car. It was very quick, but large and unmistakable. There was no way this was a trick of the eye.

Chloe picked up her phone, her eyes still on the mirror, and dialed for Ethan at the cottage. Nothing. There were no bars.

She heard it this time: movement outside. A crunch of snow and a breaking of brush heightened by the winter stillness. Quickly, she reached around to lock all the doors. Her own, however, seemed set against being fully closed again. The thick layer of ice that had formed the night before was keeping the door from locking back into place now.

She tried to start the car again. Whatever was out there—an animal, most likely—surely couldn't open doors. But windows were made to be broken.

With every turn of the key and with every dial of the phone, she felt watched. This was not a "feeling." This was instinct. Chloe's career had depended on her being aware of her situation, of her surroundings, and of possible danger. She kept her eyes open as she worked, and at last she saw something clearly. A solid dark mass was half hidden behind a large pine tree some distance away. It moved very little, but when it did, the movement was discordant with the pine's.

"Oh God," Chloe whispered. "I'm being waited out."

"WHERE AM I?"

Ethan woke with a breathless start. Icy teeth sank into his fingers and the back of his neck. His ears screamed in hellish pitches at the sensation of snow. Above him, the sky was a disinterested and sunless gray, yet it still caused him to squint as he stared into it. He wrenched, seizing as the ice and snow melted into his clothing. The fresh pain of the ice made him cry out.

His disorientation was slowly passing. He was outside the cottage by the old barn, lying on a large, flat boulder that had apparently been used to cover the well. He couldn't have been out there for too long. There were still patches of his underside that had not been dampened by the snow, and his skin was a blushing rose rather than a blistering red.

Ethan stood and looked around him, his mouth agape, his eyes adjusting. He noticed his were the only tracks in the snow, though he couldn't remember stepping outside the kitchen door at all. He couldn't remember anything past looking out the kitchen window. There had been a boy, hadn't there? A boy who resembled…

Jeff!

The cottage door was wide open as Ethan stumbled back inside. There had been a boy. He had been as clear as day, though now his features were becoming blurred in Ethan's memory. The boy began to resemble Jeff less and less. And where were the boy's tracks? There were only Ethan's.

A wheezing and coughing came from the couch. Jeff was turning colors as if choking on something. Ethan leapt to his brother's aid, ready to dislodge whatever was strangling him even as he himself was still shaking off what had happened to him. Jeff was turning a pale blue as Ethan lifted him for the Heimlich maneuver. Ethan was panicked and sweaty as Jeff's chokes began to turn into dying gasps.

"Come on, Jeffy," he said, a sob welling up in him. "Don't do this." A cold sticky sweat covered him like marsh humidity.

Suddenly, Jeff inhaled, his mouth wide, and he let loose a slight scream. He was breathing again, though his eyes were still shut to the world. Ethan watched as his brother's color returned. Only then did he allow the sob that had been accumulating in his lungs escape. It nearly deflated him as he slumped onto the couch beside Jeff.

The coincidence of him waking up in the snow and his brother nearly choking to death was too much for him. What had he seen, and more importantly, why had he gone outside after it? He didn't want to think about it. It was much easier to believe that Chloe was insane. He put the heels of his hands to his eyes and rubbed.

Jeff began mumbling in his sleep. They were incoherent strings of words for the most part, except once. Jeff, in a voice as clear and bright as sobriety, said, "No! You can't come in."

Ethan leaned in closer to hear. "What, Jeff? What are you saying?"

"No!" Jeff screamed.

The force of the scream and the surprise with which it took Ethan threw him off the couch to the floor. He gathered himself again, standing slowly while instinctively brushing his pant legs for creases. Then, once more, he saw the boy. The one from the kitchen window. The boy was fitted into a corner the room, and he was staring daggers at Ethan. Ethan blinked, and the boy was gone. His skin crawled with ice as he stared into the now-empty corner. The boy didn't look a thing like Jeff. His eyes were much, much too wide, and that grin…. There was nothing friendly about that grin. It was the grin of a starving man. Jeff had never hungered for anything. No one in the world could have ever hungered like that.

CHLOE WAS startled and relieved when a signal finally made it through and Ethan answered his cell phone. She heard the covered panic in his own voice as well as if she had caught him in the middle of something or thrown him off a thought.

"Chloe?" he answered after swallowing back. He had never sounded pleased to hear Chloe's voice. Not until that moment.

"Ethan! Oh thank God! I can't get the car started. I'm sitting here and I can't—Ethan? Are you still there?" She shouted as if Ethan were on the other side of a very crowded room. There was no point in whispering. The black mass knew she was in the car.

"I'm here! I'm here! Listen…." There was a long pause. Chloe waited and was about to say something when he spoke again. "I saw something," he said. "Someone… in the room. I don't know who it was…."

Chloe was still watching out her window at the form by the tree. It hadn't moved and she was contemplating escape. The hairs on her arms and neck stood on end.

"We'll talk about it when I get back. Your car is shot and I can't walk to town. I'd freeze to death before I ever got there— Ethan?"

"Jeff was awake for a bit. He woke screaming."

Chloe closed her eyes to hold back tears. When she opened them, the figure behind the trees had vanished. Her heart quickened, and she gasped.

"Ethan," she whispered. But even as she did so, she heard from his end a ruckus of sudden things: The door bursting open. A wind sweeping past. Ethan dropping the phone and yelling in fright.

"Jesus—!" he screamed, and then the signal was lost.

Chloe sat motionless with the phone to her ear. Her eyes were fixed on the pine tree where the figure had stood, her heart felt ready to leap from her chest, and her voice failed her as it petrified and lodged in her throat. She was going to die. They were all going to die.

LANA COULD tell by the way he was looking at her that the man recognized her from her films. She could always sift out the film fans. There was an obsessive quality about their stares. Almost hungry. Reminiscent of the eyes of Wicker. Whoever this kneeling young man was next to Jeff, he was a fan.

She quickly closed the door behind her as a tourniquet to the wind. She had been standing outside in the scathing cold for a while, watching the cottage, working up the courage or guile to enter. If Chloe and Jeff were in trouble, which she was certain of, there was nothing else she could do but come face to face with her own dread. Something good needed to come from this place and its ferocious history. So even as she felt a fever rising in her from the indifferent care of her own body, she stormed into the cottage so that Jeff might recover.

Ethan stood, looking unsure as to how to respond. "He's sick" was all he could manage. His face was a confused mess of emotions: grief, angst, guilt, and finally, awe.

Lana studied the dimly lit cottage, a place her daughter had loved and Michael had labored on but was foreign to her. A place from the outside that she saw as nothing more than a babysitter, then a nightmare. Every wall and piece of furniture stared at her, judged her and sneered. She felt the nightmare. She knew it was observing her. In her dreams, the nightmare took the image of a googly-eyed boy sometimes. Only eyes as big as his could see all that she had done and all that she hadn't. She almost apologized to the cottage, but stiffened up. This was not the place to fall into distraction. There was a fan present.

"Who are you?" she asked Ethan as she knelt beside Jeff and felt his forehead. She realized she looked a mess. Her bird's nest of hair hadn't been brushed but was pulled back by a limp barrette. Her eyes sat atop swollen bags of flesh.

"Ethan. I'm his brother. You're the actress?" His hands clenched and unclenched in nervous excitement.

She gave him an oblique glance of bother. "I was."

Jeff was burning up. She inspected the scratches on his face and arms.

"We don't know why he's doing it. I've put salve on it, but…."

"Little good it will do him. His problem is deeper."

"You know what's wrong with him?"

"I've seen it before." She stood, her eyes still on Jeff. "There's nothing you can do for him. Not if you can't get him away from here."

"From the cottage? What's the place have to do with it?"

"Don't be stupid."

Ethan was struck by the words as if Lana had physically assaulted him.

"He's fighting on the inside," she said.

"But we can't get off the hill. There's nothing we can do? Nothing at all?"

Lana finally gave him her full attention. "There may be one thing. But I'll have to go back up to the big house. There's a book there that may offer a solution."

"A book?" Ethan was incredulous. Lana saw his admiration for her disappear as clearly as if he had spat it out on her.

She couldn't believe she was going to do it herself. She had sworn off the book after the incident with Chloe, but she had to reach beyond that fear. Reach beyond and into another world. A world she herself had not believed in until recent years.

"Keep doing what you've been doing," she said. "Keep him comfortable. I'll do what I can. And let's hope that he keeps fighting."

"Wait!" Ethan pleaded.

But she was already outside again, and with the shutting of the door, she knew something else had come with her. She stood still on the porch momentarily, steadying herself by the post. "You're coming too, then?" she said aloud.

Only the wind answered.

She swallowed. "So be it."

Over the years, Lana had pieced together an interpretation of the events that had happened in her absence from Bad Luck Hill that mirrored what had actually occurred almost perfectly. Clues had come to her in dreams and memories. She had studied the past, those last few weeks before she left to make movies, and had seen, in her studies and memories, things she had not noticed at the time they were actually happening. The scratches on Michael's arms. The way he stared into the well, ignoring Rebecca as she played. The way Rebecca carried on conversations with the air. The way she referred to an imaginary friend as "the rascal" and said he wanted her to do mean things. And then there was the feeling in Lana's own gut that told her to stay away from the cottage. At all cost, stay away. To go in would be tantamount to an invitation. Why hadn't she relayed this feeling to Michael or Rebecca? The guilt was enormous.

So, as she walked back to the big house, an invisible companion near her breathed malevolence into the wind and her interpretation of events played like a film in her mind:

Michael must have been staring down the well again, scratching at his arm. That's the only way Rebecca could have wandered back to the big house without him knowing. She would have asked, of course, but he wouldn't have heard her. His mind was falling into the dark. If he had heard her, he would have certainly gone with her. He adored the girl.

Lana saw her daughter skipping up the hill, singing as little girls in horror films do right before tragedy befalls them. Before they're drowned by monsters. Lana saw Rebecca waving from atop the widow's walk at Michael, trying to get his attention. Yelling for him in play. His back was still to her, shoulders hunched as he continued staring down, down, down.

It was her scream that must have woken him from the dark. He could have done nothing to save her from the fall. Her body lay limp and broken on the lawn. If he ran fast enough, maybe he could save something of her. Keep her last breath from escaping. But the reality of the moment took hold of him as he cradled her in his arms.

And yet there was movement in her body. It jerked and her eyes sprang open. This Lana had seen in a nightmare. Rebecca's eyes were rolled back in her head, yet she turned to look at Michael. He was horrified by what he saw. She smiled, but it was unlike any smile she had given before. It was too wide of a smile. It distorted her delicate features to that of a growling bobcat.

At once, Michael dropped her body and stood, backing away. "Don't do this!" he shouted. "Leave her!"

But the small broken and twisted body of the girl stood as well, the grin intact and the mouth spilling bile and blood.

Slowly, she began to lurch toward her father. Each step was a struggle. Her ankles rolled and the dying nerves in her arms caused them to twitch and spasm. Her head pitched back and forth, side to side, on her broken neck and a giggle came from her throat of such drunken greed that it was predatory. Michael could not move.

She threw her body at him as if pitched from the earth, her bobcat mouth wide. He pulled back and then struck out, leveling her. She struggled to stand again and began to sob. He knew it was not his little girl who now cried before him, but the sobs still broke his heart.

"I'm sorry," he said. "I'm so sorry."

Beyond his better judgment, he reached out for her. She napped like a vicious canine, nearly taking a finger. She moved on him faster now, until she had him cornered on the cliff. There was nothing for him to do but play the game out. This thing didn't want the body of a dead little girl. It wanted his body. With Rebecca's corpse, it only wanted to play.

Rebecca jumped at him, and he grabbed her little, broken arms, swinging her around until he lost his balance. Stumbling back from a near fall to the rocks below, he let go of Rebecca's arms and saw her body once again go limp as she fell. It lay broken for a second time on the shore. Broken, as was his mind as he cried out for her.

It was almost immediately that the itching began again. The burrowing.

"She fell," Michael had told Lana over the phone.

That's how Lana had found out her little girl had died. She did not break down weeping, as the scene required, but matter-of-factly gathered what information she could from the broken man on the other end of the line. It was like taking directions to some place new. She then booked a flight home and traveled there in near silence.

She half expected Michael to be standing there beneath the big house, beside the small casket that held Rebecca. Strangely, she was hoping for it. But the girl had been buried in the garden out back. Their service was small. Lana never responded to inquiries from Hollywood friends about her daughter's death. It took no time at all for her to completely cut from her life every acquaintance she had ever made.

Before Lana had even arrived home, the rumors were already rampant in Wicker. Michael had beaten the young girl, some said. No, it was sexual. No, it was all Lana's doing. It was voodoo and devil worship and zombification. The people ate it up like soup. They licked their lips at every word.

The big house was quiet after that. Lana and Michael slept in the same bed, but they never touched again. Rebecca's room was visited daily and cleaned often at first. It was only after Michael left that Lana smashed the room and nearly every toy in it to bits and bits. They both thought that they should move out of the big house to some place new, but neither wanted to be the one to say it. They were too spoiled for fresh starts.

The rumors were working their way into their heads as well. An accidental brush of the hand from either of them was now painful. Michael's appearance took on a more sickly look with every passing day, and he screamed in his sleep. He bled from his marks and sweated in fever. One day, without a word, he moved down to the cottage. Lana watched him from the telescope on the widow's walk as he peered down into the well every day. Down into darkness.

She rarely saw him after that and had begun to miss him, when, on one restless midnight, she awoke to see him standing at her bedroom door like a detached shadow. She had no idea how long he had been there, but the light from the hallway proved it was Michael by his silhouette. She stared at him, saying nothing until at last he moved for her with a growl. His were not the moves of a seducer, but those of a rapist and murderer. She had played this scene before in a few films.

She grabbed the lamp on the nightstand at her bedside and bashed him on the head. He stumbled back and fell to the floor, holding his head. Lana rose quickly, running for her bureau and grabbing the small handgun that lay buried beneath her sweaters.

"Is this what you did to her?" Lana screamed, pointing the gun solidly at her husband. "Is this how you killed her?"

Michael looked up at her. She could see his face now, he having fallen into a spill of moonlight near the window. His eyes were wide, petrified. He let loose a moan that grew until Lana thought she might cry herself.

"It wasn't me!" Michael shouted. "It was him."

Quickly, he rose and ran from the big house. Down the stairs with a tumble and a fall. Out the front door and toward the cottage, screaming and tearing at the air. Only then, as she watched him fade into the night, did Lana begin to shake and mourn. It would be the first of many nights of mourning.

It was that very night that Michael disappeared. She thought he had run off and left her for good. She did not suspect he had killed himself to save her from a demon. Who thinks such things? Screenwriters and novelists. Not sane people. Not real people. For years she waited for Michael to return just the same. Whether that be to kill him or love him, she was not certain. She regretted not sharing her grief with him when they were together.

Lana Pruitt regretted many things.

SYBIL

SHE HAD to get out of the car. What else was there left to do? If whatever was watching her meant her any harm, Chloe assured herself, it would have acted by now. Besides, maybe it had lost interest in her and moved on. She could no longer see the figure, though the feeling of being a fish on a hook had not left her.

The fact was, if she stayed in the car, she was as good as dead anyway. Her layers were insulating, but they had been quickly thrown on. Her teeth were chattering from both the cold and the fear, and her breath was a thick soup in the air.

Chloe needed to get up the hill to the cottage. Something startling had happened while she was on the phone with Ethan. Jeff had woken up, Ethan had seen something, and then everything went dead. She was on edge to find out what was going on. She should never have left Jeff alone. She should have insisted that Ethan go. After all, when Jeff woke up, she was certain it was her face that would be the most comforting. Not his absentee brother's.

She carefully pulled on the door handle. Broken ice from the door's edges crackled and fell to the ground. Even that noise made Chloe cringe. It rang like cheap Christmas decorations. Once outside, she needed to be ready to run faster than she had ever done. That meant keeping to the trail she had come down on and not being scared from it by a pursuer. Her heart echoed down the creek bed. Her chest ached from its pounding. Her breath sent up signals.

Finally, she gritted her teeth and leapt from the car, not even bothering to slam the door behind her. She felt she was barely moving at all, though she saw covered rocks pass below her tread. She was near the bank of the creek when she heard the clamor of sliding rocks behind her. The sound was enough to break her momentum and jar her attention. Instinctively turning her head in the direction of the sound, she stepped on a loose stone the size of a platter dish. It slid out from beneath her and she fell, unable to protect her head in time from smashing into the creek bed.

She lay there, dazed and fading. What had happened? Things around her dimmed and blurred. Something was chasing her. She had been right. But what was it? Before she passed out, she saw a large dark mass appear in the corner of her vision, and it was getting closer.

LANA STOOD at the door to her library. The book lay closed on its table, expecting her. She had not touched it since that horrible evening with Chloe. How foolish the idea was now. To think that she, as an actress, could play the role of priestess. It was beyond her range. She could admit that failing now. There were certain things she just could not do. Certain parts she could not play.

The house felt different. She noticed it upon entering. Had it—that name given to undefined horrors—entered with her? She stared about the room, feeling the prickle on her skin like plucked violin strings. It was as if a dankness had settled into the place. The air was no longer free and clean. And yet she did not feel as pressed as she had been in the cottage, where whatever had followed her most certainly resided. Perhaps it only watched her from the window. She walked slowly forward.

Something inside her said, *It's all led here. Everything you never did.*

And what was that? she wondered. What is "everything?"

Of course, she knew the answers. "Everything" consisted of Mother, Lover, and Friend. Those roles she hadn't managed to fulfill quite as notably as the characters she portrayed on film.

And the worst part was, now she could not apologize to those she had wronged. Rebecca and Michael were memories in the mind and paintings on the walls.

Yes. At the window. She could see a vague form there if she did not look directly at it. If she turned her head slightly to one side, she could see it, a spindly thing, waiting and watching her. When she sat down in front of the book, she glanced up once to see if she could catch a proper view of her haunter, but saw nothing. Yet the fear climbed inside of her. She was not quite so easily lost to this spirit.

There was a specific spell she had seen in the book. It was a long time ago, and she had passed it over with a quick glance. She remembered that the spell had troubled her even then. That was the reason she had not dwelled for too long on the page. Her stomach had grown queasy, and she had quickly turned to view others.

But now she needed it and the hours were fading. Jeff, she was certain, could not keep fighting. He was nearly beaten already from the look of him. And after that, who knew what would happen. Jeff would no longer be the man she had met just weeks earlier. He would not be the man Chloe had married. He would not be a man at all.

Possession is nine-tenths of the law.

Lana had played a possessed woman in a film once. One of her box office disappointments. The script had looked good, but the director had slaughtered it. He had edited it to pieces in the manner of a music video. The character Lana had played, instead of being a woman in a crisis of faith, became a bloodthirsty whore.

As she flipped through the book of spells, she was reminded of the many horror scripts she had been sent over the years. A woman reaches a certain age and over half of the film scripts sent to her are horror. The films she'd agreed to do weren't particularly well-received when they were made, but they paid lucratively. And Lana could act the hell out of a horror script. Even a bad one.

"If you can't give them Clytemnestra, you give them camp," she always said.

And this book…. This script. She could get an award for it. She would get an award for it. But my, it was thick! How would they ever get it finished in time?

She looked to the director for assurance. At the window… the window….

She massaged her eyes. She wasn't on a film set, and the reality of the situation bit her like the wind. She was in her very own library, and this was all happening.

"Keep looking," she said. "You are the heroine here. Not the victim. You've never been good at playing the victim."

CHLOE FELT herself being dragged over the creek bed by her arms. Her body slid along the iced-over rocks with ease. Her eyes flickered open intermittently but never long enough for her to see where she was or what was happening to her. Her own breath echoed inside her and sounded to her as if it were being broadcast on a loudspeaker. Whatever was dragging her held tight. She heard a faint voice, but that only let her know she was in the company of another human being. It did little to calm her semiconscious apprehension. She could, however, ascertain it was a woman's voice. Deep and abrupt, the voice pitched and stressed certain syllables as something of utmost importance was imparted to Chloe. Something she could not understand.

The dragging stopped and Chloe felt herself being pulled and lifted upward. The woman was very strong, and Chloe's cheek rested momentarily on a thick pelt. A fur coat. She heard the squeaking of leather seats and realized she was back in Ethan's car. The woman was still speaking, but Chloe could not make sense of the words. Instead, their rhythm lulled her into a deeper state of detachment and, finally, sleep.

When she opened her eyes, she saw the cottage, though not in any form she had known it. She was standing by the uncovered well, only it wasn't winter. The snow had all melted away. Leaves were in the trees being rustled by the breeze and birdsong filled the air. The sky was a faded blue—too tired to go any deeper than that. The wind was gentle and played rather than bit. There was no stone near the well, and the barn was freshly painted in bright blood red.

Beside the cottage, waiting for Chloe to notice her, was a woman Chloe had never seen before. The woman's face showed signs of distress. Dirt marked her cheeks and forehead. Her hair was twisted into an untidy bundle, and dark circles outlined her darting eyes. She wore a simple dress like those worn by farmer's wives in decades past. It was stained and torn by time and use. In her hands, she held a length of chain.

She took the stone away from the crawl space beneath the kitchen and, with a nod, gave Chloe permission to follow her. She disappeared under the house with the chain rattling alongside her, kicking her way in the dirt like a lizard. Chloe followed the woman into the dirty dankness without thought or control of her actions. Curiosity is bait for the dreamer.

Chloe crawled through the dirt, past foundation posts and cobwebs. Over rocks and archeology. The woman had vanished from sight, wriggling invisible somewhere in the dark. Chloe pressed on. There was still a pinch of light coming from the entrance through the crawl space, allowing Chloe to see an obstruction in silhouette just ahead of her. The dreamer's curiosity took over and she reached out for the object.

Bones. Those of the woman, with one hand chained to a foundation post, the fingers frozen in a gesture of agony. Chloe recognized the ordinary pattern on what she could see of the dress and was thankful she could not see the face with more clarity. She began to inch slowly away. To crawl backward with her eyes still on the dead woman. But the woman's free hand rose swiftly and grabbed her before she got very far. The woman held to her tightly, the bones of her hand crackling with the grip. Half of the face could be seen now. Flesh still rotted there, but the woman's tired eyes were long gone.

She moaned in self-pity. "I did what I could," she said.

The frightened voice made Chloe itch. This was the mother! This was why Chloe had felt a familiarity with the woman. They had shared her body at Lana's ill-planned séance.

"What I thought was good. He cannot have us if we bind ourselves to death. He wants… he wants… he wants more flesh."

At that, the woman loosened her grip on Chloe and lay back in her original position of agony in the dark, as if she had not moved out of that pose. "At night I hear him dance above my head. Dancing in my kitchen, so glad that I am dead."

"Who?" Chloe asked. "Who does this?"

"Why, it's my Elling, my spawn, my little dish, and never an angel child more devilish."

"Who's Elling?" Chloe asked. But the woman did not speak again, her rhyme now having gone the way of her reason.

Chloe reached out and shook the dead woman, but only darkness came. "Who's Elling?" she repeated.

And a voice, as large as thunder, came out of the dark, ripping Chloe from her dream and back into the light. "Elling?" the voice said. "He's my brother."

Chloe was in the backseat of Ethan's car, wrapped in heavy furs. Her head lay on the lap of a large woman similar in features to the woman Chloe had seen at the cottage, but with a broader and more masculine face.

"Are you ready to listen now?" the woman asked irritably. "I have something you need to hear, and we haven't got the time for me to keep repeating things."

CHLOE SAT up too quickly. She ached from the fall, and she felt the forming knot on the back of her head. She closed her eyes to keep from spinning.

"You took quite a fall," the husky woman said. "When you get out of here, you should see a doctor about that head of yours."

Chloe put two and two together. The woman, the heavy dark furs. This is what—or who—had been watching her from behind the pine and who had frightened her so badly. She wanted to be angry but came up with only exhaustion.

"Who are you?" she finally asked in as irritated a voice as she could muster. "And what are you doing out in this weather, for God's sake?"

"My name is Sybil."

Chloe's head cleared. "Sybil? The sister?"

"Yes. Michael and Elling were my brothers."

"Elling and… Michael?" She could not be more stunned. Her mouth hung open and her glassy eyes grew wide. "Michael? Lana's Michael?"

"Yes." The woman was frustrated with Chloe's lack of knowledge regarding the situation.

"But why were you stalking about in the creek? And where the hell did you come from?"

"I have a cabin just down the creek. Just that way." She gestured stiffly. "I bought it after Michael disappeared. I wanted to keep an eye on things. I never trusted that actress, and I wanted to see what she really did with—to—my brother. I was certain she had killed him."

"But she didn't. He fell down the well."

"I know that now. I've been keeping an eye on you all. But that doesn't excuse what a lousy person she is and always has been. She shoots at me, you know. Whenever I tried to talk to her in the years after Michael's disappearance and Rebecca's fall, that bitch shot at me from her perch. Lord, she thinks she's mighty, up in the air like that!" She grumbled and looked out the window for a moment. "Michael was always my favorite brother. Between him and Elling, it wasn't a hard choice to make. Where is Michael buried? Do you know? After he was taken out of the well, where did she put him?"

Chloe felt sorrow for the woman. Lana had succeeded in keeping her away from her only family, even after death. What kind of person would do that?

"He's… in the back garden. Next to Rebecca."

Sybil thought on this and eventually decided it was good. "That's a decent burial. At least he's no longer at the cottage." She peered at Chloe harshly. "You got to get away from the cottage."

"It's Elling, isn't it? He's still there."

"Oh yes. He's still there. Truthfully, I never believed in that spooky mumbo-jumbo garbage. Not until years after I first left the cottage myself. But one night I snuck up there. This was a few years before the actress bought the place or even knew it existed. I just needed to see it again. I just needed to. I don't know why. No one had lived in the place for ages. But that cottage… it speaks. It creaks in a language of its own."

"The kitchen is the loudest."

"I saw him briefly then, my brother Elling. He was standing in a corner, watching me. I rubbed my eyes to make sure my head wasn't playing tricks of memory." She shuddered. The woman was so large it resembled a quake. "Those eyes of his always unnerved me, even as a kid. He frightened me so. He frightened all of us. He would do things…." She swallowed and looked down at her hands, gloved in thick wool. "Michael was my defense against Elling. He always said he'd get us away from Elling. From Momma."

"And did he?"

"In time…. In time, yes. He did in a manner of speaking. When he ran, that gave me the courage I needed to run away myself. But I'm getting ahead of my story, missy. Let me tell it my way."

"Sorry."

"You see, Elling was not a good boy. He might have turned out okay under other circumstances, but… I'm not even sure about that. He had a wretchedness about him right from birth, my momma used to say. He was a violent boy, and I believe Momma regretted bringing him into the world. She once said God should have taken him the moment he spilled out of her." Sybil straightened her back as if readying herself to tell a heavy truth. "I'll just say it. He was evil. We couldn't keep an animal around the cottage. He killed every pet we had, either by throwing it down that damn well or by some other more gruesome means. When we didn't get any more real pets, he went after every little critter he could snare in the woods. I buried them there behind the cottage when I found their carcasses, the ones I could get to. Every creature deserves a proper burial."

"That was good of you. I stumbled across them. Their graves, I mean."

"Elling once even tried to kill Michael. Tried to drown him in this very creek, but Momma was nearby. She loved us. She wasn't a bad momma, you see. Just a crazy one. Her love was crazy too. There were only two things Elling was ever scared of: Momma and the big house."

"Why the big house?"

"That had something to do with Momma too. Elling disappeared once for nearly an entire week. Momma was sick with worry. Not only for him but for any unfortunate thing to cross his path. That's one of the reasons we never went into town. There was no telling what Elling would do or who he would do it to. He frightened the townsfolk more than he frightened us. He was a Halloween mask on a pretty spring day.

"One day Momma found out that Elling was up at the big house. He had snuck in one night and was staying at the top, in the cupola, where no one ever went. He'd sneak down when he could—giggling, no doubt—and scavenge for food. It was only by chance that one of the servants at the big house finally went up to the cupola. I imagine they got quite a fright when they saw Elling grinning and staring back at them from behind the door. Momma beat the hell out of Elling for it, too, with a stripped tree limb. How he yelped! It was the only time I ever felt bad for him. All through that beating, she taught him etiquette. You don't enter a person's home unless asked, she'd say. You've got to be invited in. Maybe they don't want you there.

"I always wondered why Momma truly beat him so roughly. Was it really because she wanted to teach him to respect the property of others, or was it because she was afraid he'd leave her? This was after Daddy had died, after all, and Momma was always afraid us kids was going to leave her just like Daddy had. Boy, she kept an eye on us.

"Things weren't always so bad at the cottage, though. I can even remember some good times. Daddy playing his fiddle after dinner. Michael, Elling, and me having snowball fights. Helping Momma cook. That was nice.

"And from what I know, Elling himself didn't start out too bad. He'd almost died at birth, Momma said, and she and Daddy were so relieved when he finally pulled through. But then he started acting up. He bit the head off a mouse at the age of two. And then Daddy died from some strange flu. Momma said she seen it coming. She said he was saying some crazy things. She went into town and got him some special medication. She'd stir it into his soup every day, but it didn't help. He died just the same. And then Momma snapped as clear and loud as a twig.

"When Momma saw that she couldn't beat the devil out of Elling, she decided to starve it out of him. She tied him up in the barn like a dog, and boy, did he ever howl. Me, Michael, and

Momma would be sitting at dinner and have to hear that howling and crying. Elling cussed till the barn blushed red. It turned my stomach, but it didn't seem to bother Momma. Nothing ever did once she got it in her head that her way of thinking was the right course of action. Elling stayed tied up in the barn for a while with nothing to eat or drink but water and scraps of bread."

"That's what led to his death, right?"

"How did you know about that?" Sybil eyed Chloe suspiciously.

"I-I did some research on the place after we moved in and strange things began happening."

That seemed a reasonable explanation for Sybil. "The crazy fool. Started gnawing off his own hand. Momma felt bad, I guess, and untied him. He saw that as his chance and he ran. Ran right out the barn and down the well. I remember Momma screaming for days.

"Michael ran away soon after that. I think he sensed something was… wrong before the rest of us. He never said a word to me about his going. He was just gone one morning. Momma did not react well, as you can imagine. Now I was all she had and she watched me harder than ever. I half expected her to tie me up like she'd done Elling and I was on my guard for it."

"If things were so terrible, why did Michael ever come back? Why did you?"

"The same reason: family. To make amends. Elling was an evil boy, but he was our brother, and we let him down." Her eyes were heavy with the grief and guilt. "And Momma. She was a lost soul. She still is, I believe."

"Did Lana ever know Michael had lived on Bad Luck Hill before?"

"No. I wouldn't think so. Michael talked to me once—one of the few times he could—when they were just getting ready to buy the place. I thought he was crazy at the time. But now I get it. We all have to head home at some point. We all have to face the horrible things that make us who we are. We have to try and get over the falls that take us down."

"Why? Why do we have to do that?"

"It's the only way to move on. Otherwise, a person will just keep falling."

"I suppose." Chloe curled up in the fur. "And you? How did you finally get away from the cottage?"

"Loudly. It was soon after Michael left. The nightmares had started for me and Momma. We'd either wake to our own screaming or that of each other. Those were awful, nasty dreams, and I won't go into them here." She looked at Chloe. "You don't look like you could handle them. I barely could and look at me. I'm three times your size."

"You'd be surprised what I can handle."

"Maybe. Still, I'd rather not think on them. Momma had them worse than me. But after a while, she seemed to get used to them. Once I heard her talking to herself in the middle of the night. That cottage gets pitch black at night, as you know. You can't see for nothing and the silence is threatening. So when you hear a whisper through that dark and silence… well, it's terrifying. I slept in the front room of the house, as me and my brothers had done since we were kids, but I could hear Momma's whispering like she was two feet away.

"Truth be told, I knew Momma wasn't talking to herself. Not really. Like I said, I didn't believe in ghosts and the like until much later. At least, not admittedly. But deep inside somewhere, I knew that was Elling with her. Her voice shook and pleaded, though I could never really hear what she said. I didn't want to know, and I was too scared to get up and tiptoe to her bedroom door to listen. I was a big girl, and that noisy house had become unforgiving toward me. I curled up in my bed and heard fleeting words like *taste* and *sorry*. Every so often a sharp, foul word too, which was the most unsettling because Momma never cursed. I wonder if that was truly Momma at all who said those words.

"It was around that time I started to notice the scratches on her arm. Her eyes would often glass over when she looked at me, and she took to standing over the well and staring into it."

Chloe felt her stomach tying and knotting as Sybil spoke. "Did she get sick?"

"Very ill. Sometimes she was out cold for days. Sometimes she'd shake so violently I thought she was going to explode. Sometimes she'd fight in her sleep.

"One night after supper, I was taking the scraps out to dump them. Momma had been feeling better that day. It was actually not a bad day, as days went.

"Momma nibbled on some bread, then she went out to stare into the well. It was dusk. I felt her eyes on me as I passed her with the scraps. She was making me wildly uncomfortable. Wickedly so. Like how I used to feel around Elling. I tried to hurry past, to get to the woods where we dumped the leftovers— the least we could do for the forest critters after the way Elling had terrorized them. I had been thinking of running away for days, but honestly, I hadn't planned to do it on that particular night. But that was the night it would have to be.

"I heard Momma behind me as I entered the woods. I walked quicker. So did she. Before I knew what was happening, I was running. I threw the scraps to the ground and hightailed it. But Momma was quick. In no time, she'd caught up with me. The trees and the darkness had made it difficult for me to get away. Momma tackled me, laughing. Laughing just like Elling. That high-pitched noise that always sounded like a mad coyote to me.

"I felt a pain in my calf and then felt the blood. Momma had stabbed me with a small kitchen knife. She was meaning to unheel me so I'd never be able to get away. Looking back, I'm not sure if I was fighting Momma or Elling. It was probably a combination of them both. Like alternating souls running the same body, with nearly identical purposes.

"I kicked and threw her off. I might not have been as fast as Momma, but I was still stronger. She came back at me, teeth bared, and goddammit if she didn't mean to chomp down on me. I saw that for certain. I struck at her, landing my fist right across her jaw. She screamed and that nearly broke me. Nearly made me stop all the fuss and let her—and Elling—do what she wanted to me. No girl wants to hear her momma scream, especially because of something she's done.

"I was able to get up, though, and I ran. I ran as fast as I could, which, given the circumstances, was pretty fast. Momma screamed behind me. She kept calling for me to come back. That she was sorry. That she'd make me my favorite cake if I'd just come back. But I had lost her, in more ways than one.

"I stumbled around in the woods on the hill all night until I found an abandoned cabin up the creek. The one I'm living in now. I stayed there for a few evenings, daring myself to go back to Momma. I could hear her howling in the night, like she'd done when Elling fell down the well. She needed me. She was all alone and crazy, and who knew what she might do. Thinking on it, who knows what my brother was trying to convince her to do. I keep thinking of her teeth. That wasn't my momma. The knife? Maybe. She was batshit crazy, after all. But trying to bite me like that? No. Crazy as she was, she was still a lady.

"I left Wicker after about a week and promised I was never going to come back. Went into the real world, a terrified little girl, and did what I needed to survive. I made a name for myself cleaning houses, and it's been good money. I tried to never think about this place again. It was a whim of sick nostalgia that finally urged me to see the cottage once more. That's when I came up here. And then Michael got hold of me after so many years to tell me he'd bought the place. Or rather, the actress had bought it for him as a birthday present. Momma was long gone, of course. Neither me nor Michael ever knew what became of her. Michael said he was half hoping she would still be there."

"But Sybil," Chloe said, placing a hand on Sybil's forearm. "Your mother is still there. She never left."

Sybil looked at Chloe in confusion. The warning expression on her face could either evolve into extreme rage or extreme grief. "What are you talking about?"

"She's under the kitchen. She chained herself under the kitchen."

With the implication of what this meant, Sybil's eyes widened and her expression toppled over into grief. She transformed from a sturdy rock into something more delicate, and put her head in her hands and sobbed and heaved.

LUCIDITY

LUCIDITY AND awareness came back to Jeff like fresh air and clean water. He opened his eyes and mouth and breathed it in as deeply as his lungs would allow him. Ethan was there, just as he had been in the hallucinations. The face Jeff hadn't seen for so long still wore that cautious expression it had worn since childhood. The face of a man excluded from Jeff's limelight and forced to stand in doorways, only watching. A face under whose expression were layers of questions and accusations.

"This is real," Jeff said. He strung the words together in surprise. He grabbed Ethan's arm. "This is real!"

It shocked Jeff to see true concern for him from Ethan as his brother smiled warily. Ethan dampened a rag for Jeff's forehead.

"Welcome back," Ethan said. "Stay this time."

Jeff carried his voice like a great boulder up a hill. "I don't think I'll have long, Ethan. He'll be back."

Ethan stopped. "Wh-who?"

"The rascal. He's a digger, but he's not digging right now. Something else has caught his attention."

"Jeff…. Shhh." The tail end of a nervous swallow distorted his next sentence. "Don't talk like that. You're fine now."

Jeff squeezed Ethan's arm. "Listen to me! That little demon is coming back. He wants me, and I don't know how much longer I can hold him off. You've got to get out of here. You and…. Where's Chloe?"

"She went to get help. I stayed to watch you. We're going to get you out of here, Jeff. Don't worry."

"He's watching her. That's where he went. Fuck."

"She's… a smart woman. She can manage anything thrown at her."

"Not this, Ethan. Not a pissy spirit."

Ethan paused, trying to calm his brother. "I don't believe in pissy spirits."

"I didn't either." The boulder was heavy. "But they don't care."

Ethan looked down as if he had just been scolded or teased. Jeff recognized the look from having been the cause of it so many times when they were younger. Their mother had taken Jeff aside once and said, "You need to take care of him, Jeffrey. He's not got your strength. He has to work ten times as hard to get half as far as you. Act like a brother, dammit!"

"How is Kelton? How is the baby?" Jeff asked.

"They're good. They're real good." Jeff saw a light in Ethan's face that had never been there before. It changed the whole makeup of Ethan's face, making him nearly unrecognizable. Handsome. "Kelton is the best dad, and I wish you could meet Bug. The truth is, I've never been more content. Things… turned out far better than I thought they ever would." His eyes registered an epiphany.

Jeff smiled. A chill traveled through his limbs. One different than the chill of illness. He thought at first it was happiness, but then he felt the truth of it. This was jealousy, and it matched perfectly the face he had known Ethan by as children.

"Me too," he said.

"I'm sorry, Jeff." Ethan's face darkened once more. "I'm sorry for not staying in touch. For not trying to work things out."

"I wouldn't have talked. You know me, Ethan. You have me right where you need me right now. All I want to do right now is talk. Besides, if we're talking apologies, there's a whole childhood I might need to atone for."

Ethan did not refute this. Jeff did not expect him to. The moment accepted the words as truth. The clock took down the seconds.

"It seems," Ethan said, "both of us could use some work. I just hope I can be a better parent to Bug than Dad and Mom were to me."

"They tried, Ethan. At least, Mom did. She really did. You just didn't see it. There are things… so many things you can't see that really do exist."

"Well, then, those things need to be more obvious. I need signs. I hope Bug never has to go searching to see how much I love him. And Kelton."

"At least you've had the opportunity to be a dad." Jeff felt the familiar surge of anger toward Chloe about the child he could have raised. "Who needs enemies? In the end, your family does just fine in killing you."

"You would have been a good dad, Jeff."

"I bet you are, huh? I bet you're the best damn dad that ever was."

"A compliment?"

"No. Just wondering." He swooned. The room tilted.

"I do what I can. I try my best." Ethan seemed deflated and rose. "You need to eat something. I'll get you some soup."

"Ethan," Jeff called for him as Ethan walked to the kitchen. "What can we do? About this. About us. When we're off this damn hill, what can we do about me and you?"

"What do we want to do about it, Jeff? We're too old to change now. Much too old for that, I'm afraid."

ETHAN LOOKED through the ancient refrigerator that had come with the house, an old white lump of a thing that was better referred to as an "icebox." The food had yet to spoil and, given the temperature outside, would probably be just fine for days to come.

Ethan's hands moved mindlessly over the few items on the shelves, some vegetables, some cheese, a bottle of milk, all bought on Chloe's last trip into Wicker. The floorboards creaked loudly as he made his way to the cabinets. There were cans of soup there. He had seen them when he had arrived and had gone searching for something to drink so that he might tolerate Chloe. Jeff would need to make do with cold soup from a can since there was no way to heat anything up aside from setting the cottage on fire. He looked through drawers until he found an old can opener.

For a moment, there in the other room with Jeff, Ethan had felt happy. The thought of home, of Kelton and Bug shot waves of joy through him. He was excited about the prospect of finally sharing that life with his brother. And there was something else to it as well. At last he had something Jeff did not. He was finally the showiest kid at show and tell, and he was so proud to be it. But….

But. There was always that word, stunting the growth of a sentence, a thought, a life.

But, when he saw things the way they truly were, when he was able to step back and really perceive his relationship with his brother, he knew nothing would ever change. He didn't know if he wanted them to, and that was the great punch in the gut of the whole situation.

Comes a cry, But he's my brother!

Comes the truth, So?

Out of habit, Ethan looked at his cell phone. To his surprise, there was a signal. Only a single bar, but there was a signal. His heart sped up, and he simply stared at it momentarily. There was a decision to make. Should he call for help or use this moment to get hold of home? There was family on both sides of the argument, and one would have to be ignored.

The phone only rang once before it was answered, a voice barely discernible over the line. "Ethan!" Kelton said. "What's going on? Where are you?"

Ethan dropped the can opener upon hearing Kelton's voice. "I'm at the cottage. There hasn't been any signal since I got here. God, I've missed your voice!"

"No signal? … much now either."

"What? I didn't get most of that. Doesn't matter. Listen. Where's Bug?" Ethan did not move a muscle, fearing he would lose the connection if he did.

"He's right here … crying a lot … fine now."

"Give him a hug and kiss from me. Tell him I love him."

"Ethan, what's wrong?"

"Just tell him I love him!"

"Okay. I will. Ethan?"

"I love you, Kel. You know that, right? That I love you and Bug. I love you more than anything in the world." It was a good-bye. The realization only just hit him: this was a good-bye.

"Ethan?" Even over the weak signal, Kelton's voice was strung thin with emotion.

"I love you, Kel. Things will be different… when I get home. I promise." There was no response. "Kel? Kelton?"

The signal was lost, and slowly Ethan put the phone away. He stood at the kitchen counter for a moment, replaying every crackled word he had heard Kelton say. Every intonation and slice of concern. He hoped it all went through. All the love. All the I love yous. He so wanted to hear Bug. Just a giggle would have made things better. But now, in the course of a single night, that life seemed a fiction. Something a million miles away from where he was.

He wiped his eyes and opened the soup can, pouring the sloppy beef mess into a bowl. He got a spoon from a drawer and took the meal to Jeff.

"Who was that?" Jeff asked.

Ethan was shaken that Jeff had heard him. He was caught.

"Did you get hold of someone to help us?"

"I did. Yes. Someone to help."

"Who?"

Ethan sat the bowl on the coffee table in front of Jeff. He felt his gut festering with guilt. "I got hold of the local law enforcement. I don't know if they heard me well enough, though.

Probably not. They probably didn't hear me well enough. Here. Have some soup."

Ethan lifted the spoon to Jeff's mouth.

"Your hand's shaking, Ethan."

"I'm cold," Ethan said. "It's chilly in here."

CHLOE GOT out of the car, having sufficiently, if not completely, recovered from her fall. Sybil offered her one of her thick furs, but Chloe declined. A coat such as that would only slow her down as she made her way back up the hill. She trusted in the gear she wore that had seen her through those dreadful adventure tours in the Himalayas and the Sierra Nevada before she had decided against any cold-climate gigs.

Sybil stood beside her. The painted-white scene around them was of desolate isolation. There could not have possibly been another living soul for miles around. If either of them were to scream, the world might crack apart.

"You should come with me," Chloe said. "You could get some food."

"No," Sybil said bluntly. Her voice threatened the fabric of this delicate world. "I'll never go back to the cottage. Never in my life. I only came to see Michael's grave. To maybe convince the actress to bury him someplace else."

"You don't think she would ever agree to that, do you?"

"No."

With that, they took leave of one another. What more was there to say? They were not friends. They were passing souls. On a normal day, hundreds of souls passed each other by without so much as a nod or a smile. Human beings were no longer novelties on the world stage.

Chloe began the climb up Bad Luck Hill. Sybil told her she was going to head down to Wicker and find some help for them. Chloe looked back once, but Sybil had already vanished.

She checked her cell phone. Her brow furrowed. Was it a trick of the eye, or had she just seen a signal? There was none now, but she could have sworn there was a bar there for the briefest of moments. If so, she hoped Ethan saw it too and had put it to good use.

THE CAR blocked the path. Sybil cautioned herself around it and started on the trail through the woods into Wicker. She had taken it many times as a child when her parents needed something from town, and though grown over now and thick with fallen branches, it would still be a shorter route than taking the road.

Ethan's car moaned and wobbled as she leaned on it for support in getting over onto the trail. Once there she made haste. The hill here was only slight in its descent, but Sybil began to walk briskly from the first step. The breeze hissed at her. He was watching her.

"Leave me alone, Elling!" she shouted, picking up more speed. "Leave me be!" Her voice had risen at least an octave.

It was like when they were children and he would terrify her in the woods. She would run, screaming and breathless, but he would eventually catch her and tie her up. He would tease her with words like "Momma's big girl," and he would do terrible things. Then he would make her watch him do those awful things to the animals. The memories were worse than the actuality, she thought. They were colored with emphasis.

"Leave me alone!"

The woods were no longer quiet. They were screaming past her as she ran. Branches slapped her face and tendrils tripped her up. She dared not look back. He would be right there as clear as day and in the flesh, his eyes as big as baseballs, his mouth like a rotten melon rind.

She was a little girl in the woods again. Running from Momma. From Elling. Terrified and alone and no big brother to look out for her. Michael's gone. All gone. He had run away and left her again.

She heard a voice—a giggling whisper from behind a tree—say "Don't worry about Momma. Momma's fine just where she is."

Sybil wasn't sure if it was the startling voice that caused her to fall to the icy ground or if something had reached out and tripped her. She felt as if she were back in the moment when Momma had attacked her with the kitchen knife. On the ground, she heard only her own frantic breaths. The woods had stopped screaming at her. She looked around for Elling in the stillness.

"Where are you?" she challenged with hot tears rushing down her face. "Elling!"

Up the trail, down the path she had just come, she heard the caterwaul, metallic and scraping and rushing toward her. The brushing and breaking of limbs filled the woods as something pushed by them at an increasing speed. The car had been loosened from its perch and was rolling toward her down the trail.

Sybil gave a cry and tried to stand, but her furs and her weight would not let her rise as quickly as she wanted. She tried a second time, her breath as laden as her weight and her heart pumping too fast. On the third try she succeeded, but it was of little use. Upon getting to her feet, the car was there. She could only watch in terror as the car hit a bump and reared up like a great bear over her, coming down with a breaking end.

ALL THE CHANCE THEY HAD

IT WAS late in the afternoon when Chloe made it back to the cottage. Both the brothers were asleep. Jeff lay still on the couch and Ethan was curled up somewhat uncomfortably in an Army blanket in the rocking chair. Jeff's fever had broken, but Chloe knew he was still not in the clear. Elling would be back. This was merely a moment's respite.

She checked the fire, throwing in a log from the small pile beside the mantel. Embers flew up the chute in quick-shot glee. Ethan stirred in the rocking chair. The old chair creaked and popped at his movement. Chloe turned to see him. Ethan was watching her. His eyes looked like coal in the dim light.

"Have you been back for long?" he asked.

"Not too long. How's Jeff been?"

"He was lucid for a while, but then he fell back to sleep. He hasn't been too restless, which is good. And I got him to eat something."

Chloe saw the half-eaten bowl of soup on the coffee table.

"I take it my car is a no-go." He didn't sound surprised.

She nodded and took off her coat, flinging it to the floor. She trudged off to the kitchen to find something to eat. Ethan didn't move to follow.

As she set foot in the kitchen, the floor crept like curling bark. The chill it sent up her spine was such that she regretted taking off her coat. A "feeling" crept over her, but more than that. She "saw" as well and gripped tightly to the edges of the kitchen counter to bear it.

The wood floor curled and curled in front of her like a potato skin. Layer by layer, it was stripped and the earth was revealed.

Beneath the floor was the woman. Elling's mother. Chloe saw her as clear as if the floorboards were truly not there. She lay chained, parallel to the icebox door, unmoved and somewhat preserved by the coolness of Bad Luck Hill. The creaking of the house seemed now to have its true issuance from the woman's mouth, and it became more human the longer Chloe listened until at last it was a cry of anguish. The woman spasmed as if to rise. Chloe gasped out loud.

"Are you okay?"

Ethan's inquiry startled Chloe. He stood behind her in the kitchen door.

"You've been standing here for a bit, very still."

The floor was just a floor again. It creaked like all old wood floors do.

"Fine," Chloe said, moving slowly into the kitchen. "I'm fine." She avoided the icebox. Better to get something from a can.

"Lana Pruitt was here."

Chloe stopped her foraging and looked at him dumbfounded. "What do you mean "here?" She came inside the cottage?"

"She burst in the door when I was on the phone with you. She looked over Jeff and said some enigmatic bullshit and then left as if she had the only answer to our predicament."

"The book." Chloe walked into the living room empty-handed, her mind solving puzzles as she went. "She's remembered something from the book. I bet you anything that's it."

"What book? You're making about as much sense as she did."

Chloe felt momentarily lightheaded and braced herself on the back of the couch. Jeff was silent and asleep.

"I'll ask again: are you okay?"

"Yes. I think. I had a fall earlier in the creek. It's probably nothing. We need to speak to Lana."

"About what?"

Chloe picked her coat up off the floor and pulled it on once again. "About all of this. She may be right. That book might be the only answer."

"What the hell are you talking about?"

"She has a book," Chloe said, irritated and tired. "You know. A book, Ethan. It has pages and a cover and can usually be found in a library. A book of spells."

Ethan's mouth dropped. "Witchcraft? Hocus-pocus? Words on a page, Chloe. They can't help us."

"You're wrong. You are so wrong about that. Open your mind a little."

"Open my mind? You arrogant bigot." He rubbed his eyes furiously, then relaxed. "You know, I think you're absolutely fucking insane."

"And I think you're an ignorant asshole."

"Oh, I'm ignorant? Let's not get into the meaning of ignorance or you might feel your whole superreligious upbringing come crashing down on you."

"What the hell does that mean?"

"It means that if it hadn't been for you, Jeff and I might have had a better relationship."

"I loved him! I only wanted to do what was right."

"You're a hypocrite. You cheated on him and then got rid of the baby, and then blocked every attempt he made to come see me and Kelton. All because we had Bug. Two gay men had a baby and you couldn't deal with it...."

"I'm not listening to this!"

"And you had nothing. And you know you never will because he sees who you are now."

Chloe made it to the door before she swung and hit him. "I love him! More than you ever will. You're a lousy brother, Ethan. You're lousy family."

"At least I can recognize that fact."

He glared at her and she mirrored the expression. They both checked to make certain their battle had not woken up Jeff.

"I'm not having this fight," Chloe said, "the who loves him more fight. Because we both know who would win."

Chloe yanked the door open and hurried away. Ethan watched for a bitter moment and then she heard him forcefully close the door. She waited until she was a good distance away from the cottage before she found a tree behind which she could let her guilt and anguish properly surge.

LANA HID in the dark of the pantry with the large book opened and clutched against her breast. Her mouth was open and quivering in a manner unfitting a Hollywood star. The darkness pressed around her in the small room, the only place she could think of to run. It was in the house. It was in the library.

She had been in the library and had found the spell she was looking for. She stared at its words, at the script in which they were written, like briars and thorns. This would need sacrifice and the thought filled her up with poisoned dread. She had never done sacrifice too well.

It was then that the shadow made its presence known. She had thought it had left and had been able to research in peace. But then, like a door left wide open in a hurricane, the wind rushed in upon her. She breathed it in, and it tasted of bitter rust and dirt. The candles flickered and wisped out. Some of them, in their final frenzied dance, caught the edges of papers and maps that were tossed in the air by the sudden breeze.

"I've seen this before," Lana shouted, holding the book to her pounding heart. "You don't scare me. I've seen special effects that make this little show laughable."

She felt a scratch on her arm and remembered the marks on Michael. Something pulled at the book like a magnet. She clutched it tighter and ran through the blizzard of strewn things, dodging her way down the hall to the kitchen pantry.

Her breathing was rushed, and she was sweating. Her heart gave her a pang, the blood coursing too quickly through her veins. The book was so heavy she was having problems keeping it to her chest. The darkness reached for her on all sides but did not help to steady her.

She listened. Nothing. The house was silent, but she knew it was still there. In the library or in the halls and stalking, blowing out candles as it went. Or perhaps felling them so that they would catch the carpets or wall hangings alight and she would be burned alive.

Then she heard it. The shadow slid into the kitchen like a fog. It knew exactly where she was. Lana tensed even more. Outside the pantry door, it was waiting for her. This was a child's game. Unseen upon unseen. The door blocked what she couldn't see anyway.

Silence. She wanted to scream. To jump and shout. To do anything to break the awful quiet. Her legs quaked and her arms ached.

Then there was a creak at the door and she could stand no more. With that, and having lost the patience to hide, Lana pushed her way out the pantry door and up the stairs.

The second floor was completely dark, as was the rest of the house now, lit only by the end of daylight. All the color was gone, the hallway now draped in mourning. She went higher still. To the widow's walk.

She burst out the cupola door and her face met with the unforgiving freeze of the higher winds. The snow on the widow's walk had mostly been eaten away by the hungry wind. The sky was painted dusk orange and pink. The shock of the cold made her instinctively turn back for the door. The pain in her arm caught her breath in her lungs. And on the stairs she saw long shadows sliding. She heard a methodical climbing. The dusk light pulled the shadows even farther toward her, up the stairs, like ink from a well spilling upward.

Lana backed away quickly. What was real became a scene. In her mind, she heard the tense strings of a film orchestra. So thoughtless was she of what was behind her, she only just saved herself from a plunge to the ground below. The book dropped to the floor and she hurriedly picked it up again lest the pages be damaged.

The pain. The pain was intense. And a shadow figure stood in the doorway, like Death but without a crooked finger or gentlemanly top hat.

Lana dodged the shadow and fell with the book against the wall. Her legs folded on her and she laid a distorted heap, her cheek to the house. She held the book, but her grip was leaving her. The book was sliding, until it rested opened, one half leaning against the house, the other half lying on her lap.

She was no longer cold. She was no longer in any discomfort at all. Even the fear had gone. She was quite certain now that if she could turn around, she would see the shadow figure was gone as well. The set was left to her. The glorious ending she always wanted. Just the right lighting. And the music. Oh, how the music howled! How the music soared!

THINGS HAD been quiet and calm, but then….

The ceiling complained as if someone was standing on the roof. Ethan looked up as he knelt at Jeff's side. He watched the invisible journey of sound until it reached a darkened corner, and then, with a furious whoosh of rushing wind and flying ash, a gale snuffed out the warmth of the fireplace.

Ethan quickly rose and ran to grab the baseball bat from the corner, the first place his mind went. When he looked back to Jeff, his brother's drained eyes were wide.

"He's back," Jeff whispered in shakes. He collapsed into a pain-ridden yowl as he began digging into his forearm again.

"Jeff, stop it! Don't…." He tried to keep Jeff from ripping at his skin, but the digging was desperate and bloody.

Ethan stood once more, the bat still in hand and held like he would never have let his father see him hold it. With purpose.

"I don't know what this is," he said, shrugging away any doubts for the moment. He scanned intensely across the room. "I don't know what you are or how you're here, but I swear I'll bring you down if you try and harm him anymore. I will see you fall, you son of a bitch."

And as if to show he meant what he said, Ethan swung the bat in a circular path around his brother, breaking and scarring furniture. Splintering remnants from past ages and pulverizing the no-goods. Somewhere he had heard that circles were good things, safe things. Maybe making one around Jeff would help.

"Take on me, motherfucker! I'll send your balls flying. I got more rage in me than I know what to do with. You'd be the perfect outlet for it!"

There did seem to be a lapse in activity. At least a stall. Jeff stopped crying. Even the wind outside hushed. But then Ethan saw the flash of a grinning face in the corner, and he heard a sickening giggle. And once more Jeff began to howl.

Ethan raised the bat and charged at the corner.

"LANA?"

The door was open. Chloe let herself into the big house. The darkness swallowed her whole as she stepped across the threshold. The last few streaks of light were rapidly disappearing from the sky and they were of no help within the house itself. Chloe felt her way around before her eyes began to adjust to the dark. She stopped at the library door. A branch tapped on the window. Books and papers lay askance, and every candle was flameless. She noticed the book was gone. The table it had always rested on, the table where her soul had been, for lack of a better word, raped, was bare but for a single large candle that had been knocked over and bled wax on the old wood. Chloe shook her head at the nightmarish memory, resisting the urge to bolt from the place.

She continued through the house. The candles were all out or, at least, on the verge gasping their final smoke trails. Chloe called for Lana once more and again was met with silence. The wind coming in from the open door rocked the dark hallway.

The stairs denied Chloe a quiet ascent, announcing to any resting spirit that she was in the house. It was her own footsteps that made her blood pump the fastest. She gripped the banister as hard as she had at any mountain climbing line. Up into the dark. Into the cold.

The second floor was empty and just as dark as the ground floor. At least she was headed higher, though. If the big house had a basement, Chloe would have refused to enter it. Climbing was always preferred to falling.

She felt the ice-cold breeze from above and realized, Of course! Of course, that's where Lana would be. Lana would watch the winter storm from the widow's walk.

Chloe did not expect the door to the walk to be wide open, though. She expected Lana to be watching from inside, at the windows of the cupola. She shook as she stepped outside and the wind blasted her like a horn.

At first she saw nothing but the snow-covered land to her fore and the choppy, cold waters to her side. It was getting too dark to see much else. But then she saw the figure of the woman, slumped against the house.

She was lifeless. Chloe knew this before she bent down to test Lana's breath or feel for her heart. Despondency crept over her and she sat down beside the dead actress. There was nothing she could do now. There was no hope for Jeff. She did not feel the need to cry about it, but absorbed it. Tried to come to terms with the weight of what it all meant. The day had been miles and miles of trying for something that could never be. She saw that now.

And then the wind sliced past her, ripping at paper. The book. It was in Lana's lap and it was opened. Chloe peered over

Lana's shoulder like a rising moon. There she saw the words written in their poetic script.

"Oh my God!"

She understood what she had to do, what Lana had intended. She kissed the actress gently on the temple and took the book from her.

"I'll be back," she said.

Her excitement grew as she raced back to the cottage with the book. It would work. It had to. It was all the chance any of them had.

OPEN

THE COTTAGE was a wreck. Ethan stood in front of Jeff with the baseball bat in his hand. He was breathing heavily and gripped the bat so tightly Chloe could see the rage in the striations in his forearm.

"What is that thing?" he asked. "Nightmares aren't supposed to be real."

Chloe moved toward Jeff. His color was ashen and his breathing labored. His pulse was faint, and he was sweating profusely. The only evidence of sentience was the speed at which his eyes were moving beneath their lids. He was dreaming frantically.

"My God," Chloe gasped.

"It started a bit after you left. It's only gotten worse." Ethan looked nearly as bad as his brother, only he was conscious to view the horrors around him. "The fire went out… was blown out."

Chloe shot him a glance.

"Now's not the time to say I told you so, Chloe. Save it for later."

Chloe leaned in and kissed Jeff on the lips. Ethan watched, but then looked away in a self-conscious manner. He let the baseball bat fall to the floor with a hollow knock.

"You found the book," he said, pointing at the large leather-bound volume at her side on the floor. "Does it have what you were looking for?"

"It does." Chloe picked up the book and took it to the kitchen, placing it opened on the counter. Ethan followed her, taking quick glances over his shoulder in his brother's direction. "This is what Lana wanted us to find. It's a containment spell."

Ethan looked over the strange print of the old book. "Where is she now?"

"She's dead."

Chloe said it with such finality and so little emotion that Ethan simply stared at her for a moment, wondering if Chloe was capable of murder.

"Shit, Ethan. I didn't do it. I found her on the widow's walk. She couldn't have been there for too long. She was still warm to the touch. In her lap, she had the book opened to this page."

"What's a containment spell?"

Chloe petted the page and whispered, leaning closer to Ethan, "It's a trap. It lures a vagabond spirit, a wandering soul, into another form. I imagine it could be very dangerous in the wrong hands."

"How do we know our hands aren't the wrong hands?"

"They're the only ones we've got. This is the only chance we've got, Ethan. It's this, or we watch him die."

Ethan then grasped what she was driving at. He swallowed. "I'll ask this anyway, though I'm afraid I already know the answer. Where are we going to find another form to trap the spirit?"

"She's dead, Ethan. She has no more use for her body. There will be no more glamorous movies. No more parties."

Ethan turned back to the living room, running his hands through his hair. "Jesus fucking Christ!"

Chloe waited in the kitchen. Ethan paced behind the couch, his head in his hands. The woman under the kitchen floor was watching. Chloe could see straight through the boards. The woman's jaw dropped, and she formed a word. *Open.*

"All right," Ethan said, coming back into the kitchen. "Let's go get her. Let's do this now before I lose my nerve."

Chloe said nothing but picked up the book with a heavy breath.

"Just leave that here," Ethan said.

"That would be a terrible idea, Ethan," Chloe replied. "Maybe the worst thing we could do."

JEFF LAY in his dream hospital bed surrounded by crumbling walls and ruins. The sky rushed dark overhead, and the horizon was unfolding like fingers reaching across the expanse. Beside him stood the rascal. It was only he who, in the end, had refused to leave Jeff's side, chirping and whispering his threats and promises. Together, they watched the sky take down the walls around them.

"You'll let me in, won't you? Won't you?"

"No," Jeff moaned. But he was not quite so sure anymore.

"You will. You're crumbling. See? Look at yourself. And there's no one left to help you. They've all run away. I scared 'em off. I'm a mad dog. I'm the boogeyman. But we can be together, me and you."

"They'll come back. People always come back for me."

"Naw. You're a mess. This time nobody wants to fool with you. You've gone all ugly."

A rumble filled the dream and what was left of the hospital fell, deconstructed rather than wrecked. The horizon was here. Even the whispering had stopped. The rascal was gone and Jeff was alone. He closed his eyes in a painful squint as the horizon's fingers reached for him.

"Peekaboo," the rascal said. "Wakey wakey, bones are gonna breaky."

Jeff opened his eyes to see he was back in the cottage on the couch. The fire was out and the place looked torn to pieces and deserted. Chloe and Ethan were gone. They had left him. But near the fireplace stood the rascal. He bobbed from foot to foot, his shoulders hunched as if ready for a fight, and his bulbous eyes glowing.

Jeff fought against his fever, falling to the floor out of his blankets and the sleeping bag. He crawled a few inches toward the door but found he was too weak to bridge the distance. He cried in desperation and fear.

The power flickered. The lights came on, and the television flashed, but only for a moment. The rascal was distracted by this brief display, however. Jeff held his head as a sickening vertigo overtook him, and then he folded into a fetal position.

The house stretched. Every fiber of wood groaned and snapped, and the sound coming from the kitchen was that of a home being torn apart in a mudslide.

"Stop it, Momma!" the rascal shouted. "Shut up and stay put!"

Jeff gagged, lurched up, and vomited. The vertigo was not letting up, and he let his head fall backward onto the floor, which only jarred him the more.

"Don't matter none, Momma," the rascal said as if answering a question. "He's gonna let me in and there ain't nothing you can do about it. The dog's done got the bone."

Jeff raised his head enough to peer at the rascal through his eyelashes.

"Oh boy! I'm excited." The boy ghost swung from side to side in an exaggerated dance. He slurped and ogled and rubbed his belly. "We'll be fed for days, me and you."

The kitchen was screaming now. Jeff covered his ears. The rascal prepared to pounce and dig through what remained of Jeff.

But the house became suddenly very still. Jeff felt the change immediately, and he took his hands from his ears to listen. From outside came a song. A chant. Jeff recognized the voice as that of Chloe. But where was she? He held his breath as the vertigo began to dissipate.

The rascal tensed and slowly looked to the back door through the kitchen. "They're calling for me, Momma," he said. "You remember that song?"

He seemed to forget about Jeff altogether and headed for the kitchen. His voice faded even as Jeff heard him say "Pretty pretty pretty...."

THE WORST part wasn't that he was doing it, but that he recognized what he was doing as justifiable. As having a chance of success at all. Chloe's lost grasp on reality—for there was no doubt to Ethan she had come completely unhinged—had somehow encouraged his own thinking. There was no way around it. Ethan had to let go of control at last. He lit a candle and they climbed the stairs in the big house to where the dead woman lay.

Lana Pruitt, once famous and glamorous, once covered in adoration the world over, lay on the floor inside the glass enclosure of the widow's walk. Chloe had dragged her in from the cold and now had come back to fetch her. Lana's face was at last serene, void of the guilt that had weighed on her so heavily.

Chloe held the book tightly still. "She looks content," she said.

"This is crazy. We're sick for doing this. Have you talked to your god about what we're doing? Would he approve?"

"Just go find something for us transport her down the hill. We need to get her to the cottage."

Ethan's mind immediately went to Rebecca's room, wherever it was. He had seen signs of the child throughout the house. Paintings and framed photographs "in memory of." If the little girl had been as beloved by her father as she was mourned by her mother, there would be something in her room. Some large, overpriced toy or toy box strong enough to transport a corpse. Guilty parents are prone to extravagance.

It did not take long for Ethan to find Rebecca's bedroom. Aside from Lana's own, it was the largest. He had expected the room not to have been altered since the accident in any way. Ethan wondered if it had even been entered since the child had died.

That's how it was done in the movies. Rooms became shrines to dead children. But the sight he came upon was something different altogether. It smelled like a tomb. The dark of the room gave great shadows to fragments of little toys. Broken dolls' heads became monsters, and scattered alphabet blocks on the floor became antiques to avoid lest they collapse and wake the demons. He could not help but step on things further, breaking them even more. A china saucer from a child's tea set went clink; the broken ribs of a small rocker went snap.

In a corner of the room, tinged with a cold blue from the darkened sky, Ethan found what he was looking for: a sled, a pretty handcrafted item with blades of pink poetry. There was a large crack shooting diagonally downward (the sled had not escaped whatever fury had happened here), but it would do fine. Ethan grabbed it.

He warily carried Lana down the stairs and placed her body on the sled, which he had put at the foot of the front steps to the big house. He took hold of the fine rope on the sled and gave Chloe one last look of disbelief. Chloe kept the candle they had carried through the house lit and led the way with the book as Ethan followed her with the sled. He was able to keep it under control despite its occasional hastening ahead on the snow and the slope. He could see Chloe had a plan, but he was not ready to ask her about it just yet. What she did say was that they were not going back inside the cottage to be with Jeff. Not at first.

Chloe led Ethan around to the back of the cottage. It was difficult for Ethan not to at least look in on his brother. Everything in his life had been about Jeff. To ignore him with a buffer of miles was a hard enough task as it was, but to ignore him when he was just yards away was torment. He could almost hear his parents chiding him.

Chloe stopped. "Bring her here. Beside the well."

"You're not dumping her in there, are you?"

"Help me move the stone away," she said, putting the book down on Lana's chest. Jeff had covered the well again when he had heard news of the snowstorm. "I know what I'm doing."

They pushed the stone off and felt a draft of damp air escape. Chloe picked up the book once more and, facing the cottage, held it as if she were going to sing a psalm from it. The book was so large she resembled a little girl in church with an oversized song book.

"I've got a new home for you, Elling," Ethan heard her whisper. And then she began to sing. To chant the words in the text.

Briars come to life, from ink to air.
Bring home the spirit that travels there.
A new home of flesh and bone contain
Here to find and here to remain.

Four lines, but said in repetition and written in thorn.

Ethan wasn't sure now what he believed. The hours had exposed to him the lies about what was real and what was not. The things seen and unseen. He saw the wind kick up and the snow whip and rise into it. If that was coincidence or the power of words, he now could not say for certain. The trees swayed and creaked with more ferocity. The screen door at the back of the cottage slammed angrily. And all the while, Chloe chanted her sticky words, each one said as if being shot from her mouth rather than spoken.

A new home of flesh and bone contain
Here to find and here to remain.

Ethan watched the dead actress on the ground. There was no movement but what the candlelight sitting on the cover stone pretended. If the song Chloe chanted was meant to do something, it had yet to happen. Or maybe there would be no sign of change. Maybe it had happened. Ethan bent lower to take a closer look at the actress. He could discern no change of state in the corpse of Lana Pruitt. He touched Lana's cheek. There was hollowness there. No life. He shuddered in awe at the natural course of things.

"I don't think it's working, Chloe," he said.

She gave a gasp and a bitter and faint cry. Ethan knew she was annoyed at his having interrupted her chanting. He looked up at her, still in his knelt position beside Lana, prepared for an argument. But he was met with a hard leather smack that felt like a brick upside his head. He staggered back and to the side. He had barely regained his balance, barely had time to see the odd glint in Chloe's eyes when she hit him again with the book.

His balance was lost now and he tumbled into the well, saving himself from the fall by grabbing at Lana's corpse with one hand and the edge of the well mouth with the other. Above him stood Chloe. She grinned down at him. A drip of saliva fell from her mouth to his hand. Her eyes twitched and pulsed in a manner that resembled breathing.

"Chloe! Help me!"

"Oh, I'll be back for you," she said. It wasn't her. That voice wasn't hers. It was pitched and uncontrolled, going too high. "I got a man to see about a course. A main course." This was followed by a cackle without meter or rhythm.

She dropped the book in the snow beside the well and lurched unsteadily toward the cottage.

"Chloe! Come back! Leave him alone. Fuck!"

Ethan's grip was weakening. His hand slipped from Lana and he desperately grabbed at the book in a plea that somehow the weight of the tome would offer him some leverage. But the book immediately began to slide toward him on the snow. His other hand was reaching its threshold of icy pain. Everything was daggers tearing into tender flesh. As the book swept past him down the well, Ethan gave all his strength to digging into the

ground with the freed hand and pulling himself up. He yelled and
swore for that strength. He kept Kelton and Bug in his mind. Once
his shoulders were above the well mouth, he pushed up with his
elbows and then was able to at last use Lana's body as a means to
pull himself out of the pit completely. Finally, he lay beside the
dead actress, every breath a step closer to a cleared head.

Jeff's cries of torment brought Ethan back to the situation
at hand. His lungs were still in excruciating pain from his self-
excavation from the well as he raced to the cottage through the
impeding snow. He barreled through the coal-black kitchen.
The cottage was screaming. Ethan was sure of it. The place was
actually screaming.

Jeff was on the floor, writhing and crying out, as Chloe
knelt over him.

As his eyes adjusted, Ethan saw the dark liquid that shocked
the floor beside Jeff before he realized what Chloe was doing.
He retched and cursed at the sight. Then he remembered the
baseball bat, which still lay on the floor. Chloe turned to look at
him even as he swung.

She howled as her already bloodied mouth cracked and
was dislocated, gushing blood of her own. He heard it splatter
the cottage. She landed across the room on her stomach.

Jeff was crying for Ethan. His words were obstructed by
the pain as he cradled his bloodied hand, now severed of two
fingers. His screams were incoherent babblings. Ethan's natural
urge was to see to him, but Chloe was still alert on the floor. He
could see her form moving. Ethan grabbed her by the ankles and
dragged her through the kitchen to the back door against her
flailing arms and wretched screams of anger. She reached for
furniture, trying to get the upper hand, but Ethan's anger was
racing and boiling hot. Chloe left a thick stream of dark blood
in her wake.

Ethan gave Chloe a final pull out the kitchen door and went
to grab her by the collar. She kicked him fiercely and he landed a

few feet away. His fear was that Chloe would make for Jeff again, but instead, she was on top of him, raging and eyes ablaze with someone else's soul. Her dislocated jaw quivered and dripped specks of blood on him even as she tried to bite him. He defended himself from her blows, but the blood—both hers and Jeff's—dotted his face and the surrounding nighttime snowscape.

In the scuffle, something fell from her mouth and hit Ethan in the face. Something blood-soaked and wet. A ring finger.

Ethan retched and threw Chloe off him. He hardly recognized the woman he saw now. In such a short span of minutes, she had become something else altogether. Something he would never have agreed to believe in.

Ethan wasted no time. He rose and ran at Chloe, who held her jaw as she rose to meet him. For an instant, for just a moment, Ethan saw the woman she truly was peering at him from behind possessed eyes. She was horrified. She was pleading and trapped. The expression made him pause just long enough to come to a realization. In that moment of connection, he and Chloe came to an understanding about what needed to be done. The spirit must remain in its new home.

He grabbed her by the collar, and Chloe was once again replaced by the presence of another more dominant soul in her body. The rage emerged like a geyser. Chloe began choking Ethan as he pushed her near the well. Every step he grew weaker from the lack of oxygen, but no less determined. She spun him around so that it was he whose back was to the well. Her grin was supreme and caked with blood and flesh. He was losing and she knew it.

In his spin, Ethan saw figures around them in the woods. People he had never seen before were watching. He knew who they were without explanation. This was Wicker. The townsfolk. They had no intention of helping him. They had climbed the hill, black masses struggling against the white snow, with the intention of seeing a tragedy.

With a final fit of self-preservation, Ethan hit Chloe in the jaw. The monster in her screamed and loosened her grip. At last Ethan was able to right himself, but as he did so, his heels backed up into the body of the dead actress.

Now he understood. Now he was truly unbalanced. As he fell backward, he reached out for Chloe. The look of surprise on her hijacked face was countered by the one of sadness in her eyes. Ethan and Chloe fell down, heads cracking against stone until they lay with their necks broken at the bottom of the well.

Two lifeless bodies. One trapped soul. The rest was quiet.

THE COTTAGE was in pieces and hemorrhaging. The blood was in a drying puddle on the living room floor and in a great long swath through the kitchen. A distinct sign, easily discernible without mumbled interpretation. Jeff followed it once he had gotten his bearings, holding his ruined hand beneath his other arm and close to his rib cage. He had passed out and slept undisturbed where Ethan had left him on the floor, and now it was morning again. The sun had risen, tricking the world into thinking all was good. All was just fine.

Jeff walked slowly, unassured. He was severely weakened by illness and the fight. He hacked and coughed, he stumbled and groaned. If he had caught sight of himself in a mirror, he wouldn't have known who it was. He had been scarred by the scratches and his color was that of sea foam. The itching had ceased completely, though, and that was how he knew to come out of the cottage.

The snow was splattered more pink than red now. Evidence of frenzied steps and sliding falls offered a clearing for him to walk. Jeff's socked feet were numb to the cold that was biting them. In fact, the world was numb and could not but be heard as whispers even if it was blaring. The truth of things was seeping in.

At the well lay the body of the actress. She was as white as porcelain. Even in death, her face now content, Jeff had no feeling for her one way or the other. He looked past her, into the well mouth, but that sense of curiosity he had first experienced when he and Chloe had moved to Bad Luck Hill was no more. There was nothing.

With strained effort, he sat on the edge of the well, his legs hanging over into the earth and stone hole. He was alone, and "alone" felt like numbness. Jeff had never been alone in his life. There had always been someone there. His parents. Ethan. Chloe. Someone to count the days with. Someone to take care of him. To tell him he was the Golden Boy.

Alone. The word echoed in silent loops in his mind and then once aloud as he called it down the well mouth. As his voice vanished into the stone, Jeff thought he heard a bumping, a knocking about, echoing back up from down below. Like something was trapped there and feverishly trying to escape. Jeff stared into the lonely darkness and it returned the gaze. And he began to cry.

FAMILY PLOT

WICKER LOVED to talk. Bad Luck Hill was the town's primary source of gossip and shock. Anything that was of any worth in conversation had always centered around Bad Luck Hill. It brought infamy to the town, which brought gawkers, which fed the economy. Rumors came down from the hill like a mudslide and Wicker was ready for them. The townsfolk had been waiting for the first whisper of fresh rumors since the new cottage owners had arrived in the fall. Wicker licked its chops all the way through the storm, and the meal they were greeted with would last them for years.

The actress was gone, apparently having moved on. Most assumed she had finally grown tired of everything and left. Only a few whispered otherwise.

She had had an affair with the young man and was forced to leave.

No. She had killed the young woman and buried her in the garden. That would explain why Chloe hadn't been seen in town after the storm had passed.

No. She had thrown herself off the cliff. After all, a body was never found.

Whatever happened, it was for the best. Wicker had grown tired of the actress. New blood was needed.

The police finally made it up Bad Luck Hill once the ice and snow began to melt. They found only Jeff at the cottage. He was sitting on the porch, his hand wrapped in thick layers of gauze and tape. His face, neck, and arms were gouged and scabbing. Yet he was more rested now than he had been in some time.

"Everything's fine," he told them after a round of pleasantries where the deputy never met his eyes. "The power is finally back on. I did hurt my hand, though, chopping up some firewood."

"Looks like you did more than hurt it, Mr. Cane. Maybe you should come into town and see the doc." A suggestion or an order?

"Maybe I will sometime."

"How's your wife? Is she doing okay?"

"I don't know. She left me. Left me high and dry." The words were emotionless, almost as if a waste of breath.

"Sorry to hear that, sir. Real sorry. I guess we'll head up to the big house to check on old Miss Pruitt now. We haven't heard from her in a while."

"I don't suspect you would have. She left too. Yep. She left just before the storm got going. Left everything she owned there in the house. Said she hated Wicker and never wanted to be reminded of it again. I'm just telling you what she told me."

"That sounds like her. Well, then I guess we'll be heading back to town. Don't be a stranger, you hear? The whole town's curious as to how you weathered the storm."

"I just bet they are."

The sheriff understood what he meant. Jeff and the sheriff understood each other quite well. There would be very little in the form of queries by the police on the hill. That's the way it had always been.

"Be careful of that well out back," the deputy said. "That's something you wouldn't want to take a wrong step into. I'd fill it up if I were you."

(Sybil's crushed body wasn't found until years later by a lone vagrant traveling No Hope Creek. The sight of Sybil's skull gave him a fright as he investigated the wreck, so he chose not to seek shelter in what remained of Ethan's car. He scavenged for anything of worth, which was little, and then moved on. By this point, Jeff was long gone from the area, having followed other pursuits. It wouldn't have mattered anyway. The vagrant never filed a report.)

When Chloe's family first came calling a couple weeks after the storm, having at last located where she had been, Jeff knew he would be dogged by them for the rest of his life. His explanation that she had left him was good enough for the time being, but questions would rise, if they weren't already bubbling to the surface.

As suggested by the deputy, Jeff took care to have the well covered. He filled it full with furniture and debris, some from the cottage, some from the big house. He made certain to head up to Lana's in the night, lest he be sighted by any of the curious trespassers he knew were there. Once the well was packed tightly with antiques and useless things (it took the span of a week), Jeff sealed it for good with the stone and some homemade cement. He tried not to think of what lay at the very bottom. Of who lay there. He could do nothing for them, but respect what they had done for him and play things out.

There were times he questioned what he was doing. Why he was lying. After all, he had done nothing wrong. He had murdered no one. But the truth was beyond explanation. No one would believe the truth. Except maybe Wicker.

Jeff finally came down from the hill a month later. It was a cool day, but dry. The pavement in town was dried and cracked from the harsh season. Life in town was pale and slow. The faces of the Wicker townsfolk were half covered in scarves as Jeff drove his Jeep down Main Street. Of course, they stared. Of course, they nodded. Some waved in jovial manners as if he had lived there all his life. He was a local star now. His life fed their imaginations and their bank accounts. They loved him.

He wished for a plague.

Jeff would have avoided Wicker for longer. He very well could have. Lana had kept a supply of food in her kitchen and pantry that could have fed him for months. But then Kelton called. He wanted to ask about Ethan.

"I don't understand. Why would he leave me?" His voice was strained over the phone. "Why would he leave Bug?"

Jeff agreed to meet him at a small diner in Wicker. Kelton was at a booth by a window. Bug was in a carrier, asleep on the tabletop. Kelton was mindlessly stirring his coffee. Jeff sat down opposite him before Kelton noticed he was even there. His eyes were those of a single parent and all the fatigue and worry that involved.

Bug slept undisturbed by Jeff's arrival. Jeff ordered a coffee and watched the baby. This could have been him. He could have been a father.

You would have been a good dad.

"You haven't heard from Ethan at all?" Kelton looked at him pleadingly.

Jeff cast his eyes downward. "No. Not since he left."

"But why? Why would he leave? Did he give you any clue?"

"I told you what happened over the phone. I don't remember much of anything. I was too ill. But when I woke up, Ethan and Chloe were both gone."

"Are you suggesting they left together?" Doubt. Accusation.

Jeff countered the expression. "That would be silly. They didn't care for one another."

"Not at all." Kelton took a relieved sip of his coffee.

"Not at all."

"I got that one call from him during the storm. I could hardly understand him. I only managed a few words actually. When we were cut off, I got hold of the Wicker police department. They said they couldn't do anything until the storm passed and the snow began to melt from the hill. They said it was too dangerous."

"And they kept to their word. I didn't see them for some time."

Kelton studied Jeff's still-wrapped hand. "You're a strong man, Jeff. I don't know how you survived it. But then, your

career trains you for things like this, doesn't it? I wonder if
Ethan would know what to do if he ever…." His eyes welled up,
and he took another sip of coffee.

"I think," Jeff said, reaching for Kelton's hand, "Ethan
was—is a stronger man than anyone ever supposed. I think he's
a man who knows what to do, knows what needs to be done,
even at great personal cost."

"I don't understand."

Jeff shook his head. "Who does? But if you need to talk
some more about all of this…."

"Thanks, Jeff." Bug opened his eyes and, seeing Jeff,
smiled. "Listen. Why don't you come stay with me and Bug? I
mean, just until things are settled down a bit. We could get that
hand properly seen to and get some treatment for your other
wounds."

"Me? Come to live with you?"

"Why not? We're both abandoned right now. It might do us
some good to have someone to commiserate with. And besides,
we're family, right?"

Jeff sat back in his seat. Family. A grin slid across his
face. What came to him then, creeping up like a head out of the
darkness, was the realization that he was still the Golden Boy.
That things just somehow worked out for him. That everything
was only ever done for him. He was a star.

He licked his lips.

"Right," he said. "Yes. That sounds perfect, Kelton. Just
perfect. I've always wanted a family."

ERIC ARVIN resided in the same sleepy Indiana river town where he grew up. He graduated from Hanover College with a bachelor's degree in history and has lived, for brief periods, in Italy and Australia. He survived brain surgery and his own loud-mouthed personal demons.

Facebook: www.facebook.com/eric.arvin.5

Simple Men

Eric Arvin

Chip Arnold is a well-liked football coach at a small liberal arts college, but his personal life is in a bit of a rut. He goes out drinking with his colleagues, gets along well with his players, and dates all the prettiest women in town—he has the life most straight men dream of. But lately none of the women he dates seem to be igniting any passion in him. Then he meets the new school chaplain, Foster Lewis.

Romantic attraction to another man is new and terrifying, and Chip just can't put his finger on why he's drawn to Foster, but it's stronger than anything he's felt for anyone in his life. Never one to back down from a challenge, Chip decides to go for it. But love is never simple, and sometimes it's a downright mess!

www.dreamspinnerpress.com

www.ingramcontent.com/pod-product-compliance
Lightning Source LLC
Chambersburg PA
CBHW060103260626
47160CB00005B/1773